MOTHER OF THE BRIDE

Kay Sheridan enjoys owning The Tea Cosy gift shop and tea-rooms. But for her, life has become quite hectic. A developer is threatening to disturb her tranquil village, and her landlord is demanding an increase in the rent of her premises that could close her down. Then her impetuous daughter surprises her with wedding plans, which will mean the return of her estranged husband. Will Kay be able to hide her unchanged love for him?

ZELMA FALKINER

MOTHER OF THE BRIDE

Complete and Unabridged

LINFORD
Leicester

First published in Great Britain in 2007

First Linford Edition
published 2008

British Library CIP Data

Falkiner, Zelma
    Mother of the bride.—Large print ed.—
Linford romance library
    1. Separated people—Fiction 2. Love stories
    3. Large type books
    I. Title
    823.9'2 [F]

    ISBN 978–1–84782–147–8

Published by
F. A. Thorpe (Publishing)
Anstey, Leicestershire

Set by Words & Graphics Ltd.
Anstey, Leicestershire
Printed and bound in Great Britain by
T. J. International Ltd., Padstow, Cornwall

This book is printed on acid-free paper

1

The girl with the flyaway hair danced down the stairs to the beat of an orchestra only she could hear. 'I'm in love, I'm in love, I'm in love,' she sang.

Kay Sheridan, waiting at the front door, her hand already on the knob, looked up and smiled. Putting aside motherly bias, there was no doubt her youngest daughter was a beauty.

And, at eighteen, the spitting image of the man who had fathered her.

Kay's smile wavered for a moment. What chance had she of ever forgetting Greg with this daily reminder?

Zoe reached the bottom of the stairs. She executed some fancy dance steps and, flinging both arms skywards with a theatrical flourish, came to a standstill in front of her mother.

'With a wonderful guy,' she finished,

the ringing notes hanging for a moment on the air.

Looks and a pleasant singing voice as well, mused Kay fondly. Every girl should be so lucky. And thinking of luck, how good it was to see Zoe so cheerful. The girl wasn't usually a morning person.

Whoever was responsible for this change deserved a medal for being a good influence. That was more than could be said for some of the previous young men vying for Zoe's affection.

'Come along, Zoe, we'll be late,' she urged, still smiling.

Good-naturedly, Zoe grabbed her coat from the hall-stand and followed her mother to the garage.

'So the rehearsal went well, then,' Kay began once they were on the road to town.

Zoe turned within the constraints of her seatbelt, her face animated. 'Oh, Mum, he is a wonderful guy!'

'Who?'

Zoe was indignant. 'Don't you ever listen?'

Kay couldn't admit it, but she didn't always listen when this daughter raved on about boys. Since she'd blossomed into young womanhood, Zoe had attracted more than her fair share of boyfriends who had come and gone with amazing frequency. They were all wonderful guys at the time.

'Of course I listen,' she lied, diplomatically. She excused herself on the grounds that it was worth a lie to keep the peace. A mother-daughter confrontation in the car wasn't the ideal preparation for the morning's important meeting with the real estate agent.

She made an effort to soothe Zoe's hurt feelings. 'Of course I listen,' she repeated. 'But you know me, mind like a sieve. Tell me again.'

Zoe didn't need any encouragement. 'Danny really is a wonderful guy. Like the song says. And I'm in love with him. Like the song says.'

Ah, thought Kay. Danny, the director of the amateur theatre company's revival of South Pacific. It was only natural that the leading lady would get a crush on her director after weeks of up close and personal contact.

She remembered her own days in the local repertory group and how attractive older, out-of-town directors were. She doubted she could recall any one of them now.

She wondered if she should ask Zoe did this Danny return her feelings. In a roundabout way, of course, so that Zoe didn't get the impression her mother was being critical. Again, she wished she didn't have to tread on eggshells this particular morning.

'Have your sisters met him?'

The young face clouded. '*Danny*, Mum, not *him*. His name is Danny.'

Kay wondered why this daughter was always so ready to go on the offensive — the other two weren't. She supposed it was to do with Zoe's age when Greg left. Thirteen was a tricky time for girls to be parted from their fathers.

She knew Zoe blamed her for the marriage break-up although Greg had been at pains to avoid recriminations. Georgy and Alyce seemed to understand, but Kay's attempts to explain to Zoe had always ended in accusations and, on her part, increased feelings of guilt.

'Sorry. Have your sisters met Danny?' she asked, carefully swinging wide in the thickening traffic to avoid a cyclist.

Mollified, and eager to discuss the man of the moment, Zoe smiled again. 'Alyce has. She thought he was something else.'

Kay knew that meant approval and felt a little more at ease. Alyce was a sensible twenty-year-old university student, the sort of girl who never gave her mother any grief. Her opinion counted with them both.

Kay didn't know why she was worrying. Zoe's enthusiasms usually didn't last long. With the opening night of the musical only weeks away, the director would be returning to wherever he came from. Hopefully, that was a long way away.

'When are you planning to bring Danny around for a meal?' she asked, looking for and finding a place to pull over out of the line of cars and into the kerb.

Zoe undid her seat-belt, gathered her coat and bag and opened the car door. 'Tonight,' she said over her shoulder as she stepped out. 'See ya.'

'Tonight?' Kay bit back her anger. 'Bye, love,' she said, raising her voice above the slam of the car door. She sat for a moment, the engine idling, watching her daughter stride across the pavement and disappear into the only office building in the village.

They really needed to talk about the meal. Whatever could she serve that would be considered suitable? Was he a vegetarian like Zoe? She sighed. If her daughter was thoughtless it was her own fault — she had spoiled her rotten.

There wasn't time to think about the evening right then. First things had to come first and that meant negotiating the renewal of the shop lease.

The real estate agent came to the point quickly. 'The fact is, Kay, the owner is standing firm on the rent increase. He says he can easily find a tenant who will pay that amount. And refit the shop and the rooms above it.

'The area is starting to move with all the new high-rise developments along the bay. And once the authorities give permission for the tavern . . . ' He shrugged.

'The tavern? But there have been widespread objections to the idea of a tavern in this little unspoilt backwater. Surely it won't get past the council, will it?'

'The developer says he will appeal to the tribunal if it doesn't. He's an outsider and not at all sentimental. He also has the means for a long, drawn-out battle against the council and any objectors. You'll have to accept that the area is changing, Kay. Going more up-market. You'll all have to move with the times, can't stand still, you know.'

Kay was horrified. She, and her customers, enjoyed the village-like atmosphere where everybody knew your name. Young and old had been vocal about keeping it that way when the rumour of the proposed tavern first surfaced.

Now it seemed they would have to put up a fight. That would mean petitioning the council when the application came up for consideration. But that was in the future, the increase in her rent was today's problem.

'But my clientele, where will they go if I have to close? To the sushi bar? I think not. My tea-rooms are a meeting place for a lot of people living on their own, the only point of daily contact for some of them.'

The agent shrugged. 'There's one answer to that. Pay the asking price.'

Kay became angry. 'You know this rent increase is astronomical and I can't pay that much and stay in business.'

'You could take it to the Fair Rents people.'

'Another tribunal? What an expensive, frustrating exercise in futility that would be.' She rose and straightened up to her full height. 'The trouble with you business people, you don't take into account the social aspects of development,' she pronounced.

The agent came from behind his desk and made an attempt to calm her. 'I'm sorry, Kay, I'm just the messenger. Don't shoot me.'

Although she knew he was right, Kay was in no mood to be placated. When she first opened the gift shop and tea-rooms, she'd been motivated as much by the need to become independent and ease her longing for adult company as she desired to create a meeting place.

She had succeeded. With a solid core of regulars, the convivial atmosphere to The Tea Cosy attracted newcomers who soon became friends with each other.

⋆　⋆　⋆

The morning rush was beginning by the time Kay reached the tea-rooms. The low hum of voices and the familiar smell of freshly-baked muffins brought a surge of pride as she stepped inside. She had built this business from nothing. How could she give it up?

She waved a greeting to the group of women bowlers gathered for their lay-day get-together in the front window overlooking the foreshore gardens and old rotunda. Later, it would be the young mothers with their sweetly-smelling babies who filled the sunlit corner.

Expertly, she gathered up several empty coffee cups as she threaded her way through the chairs and tables, greeting her customers as she went.

'I hope that's not your breakfast, David,' she quipped as she passed the man with his head buried in the money page of the newspaper.

The accountant looked up with a welcoming smile. 'You know me better than that, Kay. I've been in the office for hours by this time in the morning.'

He was right. She did know him better than that. She knew quite a lot about David Brown and he wanted her to get to know him a whole lot better, especially since his mother died and he was free of responsibility. She knew he'd given the inexperienced Zoe her temporary job towards that end.

She nodded, then looked down at the crockery balanced in her hands. 'I'm needed,' she said, moving off. Over the years since Greg had left, being needed had been her excuse for avoiding any man who became overly interested in her. With the last of her daughters grown up, it was fast losing its validity and she knew it.

Her assistant, Elien, paused in her coffee-making. 'How did you go with the real estate agent?' she asked.

Kay moved close so as not to be overheard. 'Not too well, I'm afraid,' she replied in a low voice. 'He said the owner is immovable. Take it or leave it.'

Ellen turned a knob on the machine, the sudden hiss of steam covering her exclamation of disgust. 'Rapacious landlords,' she said when the noise had died.

Despite herself, Kay had to laugh. 'Big word,' she said.

'Big pain in the neck,' Ellen replied, shaking chocolate over the cappuccino.

'How about taking in a movie this evening?' David asked, tendering his money at the register on his way out.

With a start, Kay remembered. 'This evening? I'm sorry. Thank you for asking but Zoe is bringing home her latest boyfriend.' She frowned. 'I'll have to think of what's easy to cook.'

'I wouldn't imagine it being a trouble for you to whip up something at the last minute,' he said.

'That's where you're wrong. It's a very important occasion, you know, first meeting with Mother, his first impressions of her. Zoe will kill me if I get it wrong.' Kay laughed. 'Aren't you glad you aren't young? I am.'

David didn't join in her laughter. 'You're still young,' he said.

That was the trouble with accountants, she thought. They were inclined to take everything seriously.

'I meant *young* young,' she said, handing him his change and smiling at the customer waiting behind him.

There was a sudden rush of people and all thought of the evening meal went out of Kay's head. It was two o'clock before she had time to sit down with one of her regulars, and enjoy her favourite lunch, a toasted sandwich of avocado, ham, tomato and cheese.

'I'm thinking of selling my house and moving in with my newly-widowed daughter,' confided her customer. 'She's finding it hard to manage the children on her own. Have to put the children's needs first, don't we? They are the future, aren't they?'

Children and their needs. Kay could relate to that, although in her case it hadn't been the death of their father she'd been confronted with. The girls had been her overriding concern when Greg put forward his plan to move to

America to further his chosen career of managing the affairs of professional golfers. It was where the real action was, he said.

'You can't expect the girls to be dragged from school to school in a foreign country,' she had argued with all the protective fierceness of a lioness. 'Especially not Georgy. It's been a critical year for her.'

'But, Kay, it's a lonely life on the circuit. I need my family with me,' he had protested. 'And you, in particular. I can't go without you. Don't ask me to.'

Kay still remembered her answer, word for word — it was etched in her memory. 'Well, you'll have to if you go. My responsibility, and yours, is to our children and what is best for them.'

Greg had taken offence at that. 'Don't you see, I am trying to be responsible by establishing my career so that I'll be better able to take care of you all,' he had replied, his voice hardening.

Like their respective viewpoints had.

Although it was years ago, and she had spent hours since agonising over the turn of events, Kay could still remember her bewilderment when he had gone. She had only been doing her job as a mother.

Quite forgetting her promise as a wife, he'd said.

'What do you think, Kay?'

At the sound of her name, Kay realised she'd been lost in the past and hadn't been listening to her table companion. 'I'm sorry, what were you saying?'

'I said I'm faced with the dilemma of should I sell my house,' the woman went on. 'My other daughter says I should lease it just in case things don't work out. What do you think?'

Kay switched her thoughts back to the present and continued with the conversation until her lunch break was over.

'I'll have to get back to work now,' she said. She got up and pushed her chair back under the table. 'By the way, I'm having a special presentation night on Thursday with champagne, chocolates, lucky door prizes. Will you be able to come?' she asked.

The customer got up, too, and walked with her to the cash register. 'Thursday? I don't expect to have solved my dilemma by then and left the district.' She laughed at the possibility. 'Of course I'll come. Wouldn't miss it, not when there's free champers.'

The after-school rush began and Kay forgot all about Zoe's dinner guest until closing time. She made a last-minute dash across the street to the speciality pasta shop and solved the possibility of Danny being a vegetarian by buying freshly-made ravioli and sauce.

The easy meal preparation would also solve the other question — his arrival time. Of course, Zoe had not mentioned that either and Kay didn't want to make what Zoe would call a big deal of it by telephoning her in David's office.

As it happened, there was no need to rush. It was well past their usual mealtime when Zoe and her new boyfriend arrived together.

Kay didn't have any preconceived idea of Danny Quayle, she'd been too preoccupied all day with her own affairs to have given it any thought. Never the less, the man Zoe brought forward to introduce was a surprise.

This was no carelessly-dressed, artistic youth with over-long, floppy hair. His fair hair was of medium length and obviously cut by a good stylist, his suit a modern version of the classic single-breasted suit. In fact, on the street, he would be taken for a hot-shot, thirty-something businessman.

Kay covered her surprise by asking him what drink he would like.

'Nothing now, thank you, Kay. Zoe and I have already had a drink. I'll have some wine with the meal, though.'

Kay! Such familiarity! She hoped her

feelings didn't show on her face. It wouldn't do for Zoe to realise her mother didn't like this self-possessed man one little bit.

'Zoe, perhaps Danny would like to see the garden while I get on with preparing the meal. It won't take long.'

'Are you interested in showing me the garden, Zoe?' Danny asked. 'No? Then come over here and talk to me.' He moved into the living room and occupied a couch, clearly expecting Zoe to join him.

Obviously bedazzled, she did. Like a homing pigeon, Kay was dismayed to see. What had tamed her spoiled, wayward daughter? Could this be real love?

She uncorked the red wine to allow it to breathe, set the pan for the pasta on the stove, and bent to take the salad ingredients from the crisper in the refrigerator. As she straightened, her eyes were drawn to the calendar on the wall beside it. The opening night was ringed in black.

Four weeks.

She breathed a sigh of relief. Nothing much could happen in such a short time. It would be over in four weeks and Danny Quayle would be gone. She could only hope he would be kind to Zoe and not add to the hurt when he left.

Putting aside her concern for her daughter, Kay completed the preparations for the meal.

'Is dinner nearly ready, Mum?'

Over Zoe's shoulder, Kay could see the impassive face of the guest. 'It's just that we have something we want to talk to you about.'

'And I have business to attend to in the city,' added Danny, coming forward.

Zoe had the grace to recognise her mother might be offended. 'He is just so busy, Mum,' she explained.

Busy? More like rude! Surely he could've kept the evening free for a more leisurely visit. Indignation threatened to overcome Kay's own good manners, but she controlled herself.

'Because we both work, we dine informally on week nights, Danny,' she said, handing him the bottle of wine. 'Zoe, will you take the salad with you, please? I'll bring the pasta.'

Danny Quayle became the perfect dinner guest. He expertly poured the wine, after tasting it and pronouncing it an excellent choice, complimented Kay on the salad and the luscious fruit flan she served as dessert.

'All purchased in the village,' she told him. 'We lack for nothing, despite being considered a backwater.'

For a moment, the threat of the proposed tavern that would change all that, came to Kay's mind. She quickly dismissed it.

'Now, you said you have something you want to talk to me about.' She raised her eyebrows, glancing expectantly at them both.

Zoe leaned forward, her face alight. 'Mum, Danny has — '

Danny Quayle placed a restraining hand on her arm. 'Yes, we do,' he said smoothly. 'Zoe and I would like to get married.'

2

Married?' Kay couldn't hold back her incredulous cry — it was the last thing she expected. Utter surprise and the built-up tension of the day combined and exploded into that one word.

Of course it was a mistake. Zoe's face took on a familiar mutinous look, but Danny Quayle held her glance and his expression hardened into that of a man used to having his own way. It was almost as if he was daring her, almost a declaration of war. But why?

'Yes, married,' he answered, an ingratiating smile that didn't reach his eyes replacing the implacable stare. 'That is, with your permission, of course.'

Kay's glance went back to her daughter. She marshalled her thoughts, desperate not to provoke her any further. From past experience, she

21

knew Zoe was likely to resist any opposition, stubbornly digging in the more that pressure was applied for her to change her mind.

And as for Danny Quayle, Kay had no doubts as to how he was going to react to her objections, he'd already signalled that, but everything else about him was unknown.

Unknown. It was somewhere to start.

'You haven't known each other very long,' she said. 'How many weeks is it?'

Zoe rushed in with a question. 'How long did you know Dad before you married?'

Kay felt it was a sneaky, almost disloyal blow. 'Well, that was different,' she answered, trying not to sound defensive, but knowing she'd been caught on the wrong foot. Theirs had been an across-the-crowded-room discovery of each other, followed by a whirlwind romance. It was a story told to the girls often as they grew up.

Until the break-up.

'How different?' Zoe wasn't letting up.

Kay wondered did she imagine the look on Danny's face that said Gotcha? Why was he making this such a contest of wills? Surely he didn't expect she'd be pleased? And antagonising your future mother-in-law was not a good way to start.

She answered her daughter. 'At the time he was in a steady job as the manager of the local prestigious golf club.'

It wasn't a good answer. Danny's eyes narrowed.

'Are you suggesting I'm not suitable for your daughter because I'm not a local in a regular nine-to-five job?' he asked in an ice-cold voice.

Zoe, all indignation, broke in. 'Dad's job wasn't nine-to-five. You're so old-fashioned, Mum! No-one works those hours nowadays. And anyway, it won't be a single-income marriage like yours was. We'll both be earning our own money.'

Did that mean they didn't plan on having children right away? That was a plus — Zoe was hardly motherhood material just yet. Kay fiddled with the stem of her glass, searching for more diplomatic ways of expressing her other concerns.

Of the several reasons for disapproving of the marriage, the one uppermost in her mind was she didn't like Danny Quayle. But how did you tell your daughter you thought her choice of the man in her life was all wrong?

At eighteen years of age would she have listened to that kind of talk? Luckily, she hadn't needed to; her parents approved of Greg and agreed to the marriage despite her youthfulness.

'Darling, you're really too young to be getting married. Wait a while.'

Zoe certainly knew all the right points to score in an argument. 'How old were you when you married, Mum?'

'But that was different . . . ' Even as she repeated herself, Kay was aware it wasn't a good answer either.

'How different?'

Danny had that look on his face again. Questions raced across her mind in quick succession. How long had they been planning this . . . assault? They seemed to be working as a team. Did that mean they really had something in common?

'Go on, Mum, how different?' Zoe's voice cut across her thoughts.

Kay knew she couldn't reply truthfully. Not without hurting her daughter and giving Danny ammunition. She fell back on a cliché.

'Twenty-five years ago things were easier, the economy was booming . . . even in the theatre.' She included Danny in her reply.

'I'm going to ask Dad,' Zoe said, defiantly. 'He'll understand.'

Kay felt something like relief. Locating Greg would probably take time and time was what she was depending on. Given enough of it, and after the initial enthusiasm faded, Zoe might change her mind; she usually did. It was part of her mercurial charm.

'I would be happy with that,' Kay conceded. 'Have you any idea where he is?'

'Yes.'

Despite the occasional newspaper item, she had long ago schooled herself not to take an interest in Greg's very successful career. It was the only way she'd been able to cope, but she'd forgotten the golf tournament calendar pinned behind the door in Zoe's room.

She had no doubt her daughter knew exactly where in the world her father's high-profile clients were playing at any time. Accompanied by Greg, of course.

'That would be a good idea,' she said, summonising a conciliatory manner with an effort. Hopefully, in view of the failure of his own early marriage, Greg would urge caution. Feeling more cheerful, Kay asked, 'What about coffee?'

Danny Quayle pushed back his chair and stood up. 'Thank you, Kay, but I have an important meeting in the city.

Better get your jacket, Zoe.'

Kay watched in astonishment as her daughter raced up the stairs to her room without a murmur of dissent.

'Zoe is going, too?' she asked. Obviously there wasn't to be a mother-daughter chat.

'Yes, we're a team.' Danny held out a hand. 'Goodnight, Kay, and thank you for the meal.'

A team? She'd been right, but how unromantic of him. And thank you for the meal? What about thank you for your daughter?

Zoe was following her usual Saturday routine and still in bed when Kay left for work the next morning. A last look in the hall mirror showed Kay the sleepless night hadn't been kind to her, leaving her hollow-eyed and listless.

Soon after opening, the tea-rooms filled with the regulars enjoying coffee and a muffin with their weekend newspaper. There was scarcely time to think about home matters. It was late afternoon before the last of the chairs was up-ended on the tables, and the floor mopped ready for the start of a new week.

The murmur of television as Kay opened the front door alerted her to the fact that her daughter was at home.

Hopeful of a heart-to-heart talk about marriage with Zoe, she hesitated before entering the living-room, reminding herself she needed to proceed carefully.

Her daughter was lying on the sofa in front of the television, engrossed in the programme. It was a moment before Kay realised she was watching a direct broadcast of a golf tournament.

'Oh, hello, Mum,' Zoe said, hardly taking her eyes off the screen.

Kay flopped into an armchair and kicked off her shoes. It had been a busy morning, the new line of chocolates literally walking off the shelves. Twice she'd had to go upstairs to the storeroom for more supplies.

A thought crossed her mind — perhaps the rooms above the shop could be let. That way she could afford to pay the higher rent her landlord was demanding after all. She'd ask David Brown to run over the figures when he came in on Monday.

'What are you watching?' she asked casually, hoping Zoe would say it was nothing important and turn it off. They really needed to talk.

'Dad is playing.'

Kay tensed. She usually avoided watching anything connected with golf, with the chance of seeing Greg to remind her of her loss. The pain of that hadn't diminished over the years, and, as time went on, the realisation of the mistake she'd made.

They both sat in silence, staring at the television. At last, trying not to appear too interested, she asked casually, 'Where is this?'

'It's a big charity day at The Lakes. Managers are playing against their clients.'

'But that is in Sydney.'

'Yes,' was all Zoe said.

Sydney! Greg was back in Australia?

'Here he is now,' Zoe offered unnecessarily.

The camera panned in on the still-familiar, tall man poised to tee-off. Kay didn't hear the commentator's remarks, her attention concentrated on the golfer addressing the ball. Although he was now in his forties, the lithe figure in beige pants and blue shirt showed no sign of having thickened with the years. A sponsor's cap hid his hair, and dark glasses, his eyes.

At last, he braced his legs, the gathered crowd fell silent. With a twist of his slim hips, he swung the club easily in a fluid movement that sent the ball soaring into the air.

After a moment, a distant shout confirmed its accuracy. The onlookers applauded generously.

Clearly enjoying himself, Greg lifted his cap in acknowledgement, the breeze that fluttered the flags behind him catching and ruffling his hair. Kay felt her heart lurch at the attractive sight.

Among the experts the talk then

had been that he had the personality as well as a good business head on his shoulders and would go a long way in sport management. How right they were! Zoe had proudly informed her not long ago that he now managed the affairs of several international golfers.

The cameras stayed on Greg and his big-name playing partner striding down the fairway with their respective caddies, followed by the crowd of admirers, before switching to another player.

As they disappeared from the screen, Kay shook off her past regrets and got up out of the chair.

'Coffee?' she called when she reached the kitchen, hopeful Zoe might join her. It worked.

'Any muffins?' Zoe asked, rifling the bags of food on the bench. 'I haven't had breakfast.'

Nor a shower, Kay thought with fond amusement. There was something so young and appealing about the pyjama-clad figure perched on a stool that made the idea of marriage so incongruous . . .

'No muffins left,' she laughed, expertly producing a plate of fruit. 'We'll have an early dinner, to make up for it.'

'I won't be home for dinner,' remarked Zoe, biting into an apple. 'Danny and I have a meeting with some television people.'

Kay realised this was how it was going to be from now on and wondered if the prospect of a lonely future could be one of the reasons she opposed the marriage. Did the empty-nest syndrome apply to her?

'I thought we could have a talk about the . . . ' She hesitated, finding it hard to say the word *wedding*. 'I thought we could talk about . . . ' she began again. 'Your plans,' she finished.

Zoe pushed her hair back behind her ears, her face suddenly dreamy.

'I'd love the whole works, you know, long white dress, strapless, of course, but with a train, my sisters as my bridesmaids, driving to the church in an open carriage . . . ' Her voice trailed off.

Caught up in the dreaming, and despite herself, Kay wondered what colour she'd choose for her frock. 'I'm not going to be a mother-of-the-bride in lavender or apricot georgette. No way!'

'And what about a piper? Do we know which church has a carillon?' Zoe's voice had lost its dreaming and become more down-to-earth.

Kay became more practical, too. 'Hey, wait a minute. Hadn't you better ask your father first? After all, he will have to pay for it.'

Zoe waved away the caution. 'It will be all laid on, anything we want.'

'I wouldn't be too sure of that. You'd better ask him, before you make your plans.'

Zoe leaned forward and became more earnest. 'But we can have anything we want. That's the best part of the deal.'

'The deal?'

'Danny has put forward a proposition to a television production company to film our wedding. That's where we're going to tonight, to be interviewed again.'

'Television?' The word brought an instant rush of dismay to Kay — she couldn't imagine anything worse than an intrusive camera. 'You mean the television people will come to the wedding?'

'No, no, that's not how it works,' Zoe said rather impatiently. 'Danny plans the production, the independent film company films it, with him directing and then they sell it to the television company. Haven't you seen advertisements on morning television?'

'No, I haven't. I'm usually too busy getting things ready for work to be watching television.' She had a sudden revelation. Zoe had her own television set in her room. 'Is that why you always take so long in the morning?'

Zoe wasn't going to admit anything. 'Don't they talk about it in the café?'

Kay allowed herself a smile. 'As a matter of fact, the morning-tea crowd do like to watch that sort of thing.'

And why shouldn't they? They were retired and the morning rush was no longer a part of their day.

The smile faded as her thoughts turned back to Zoe's wedding wishes.

'I don't think I could manage to organise a big wedding — '

'But you won't have to do anything. I told you, Danny will arrange everything, he'll be the producer,' Zoe explained.

Danny arrange her daughter's wedding? Had she missed something?

'Well, that's a relief,' was all she could say.

She reminded herself there was no need to become alarmed — not yet. It was, after all, a long shot.

As she understood it, Danny had to convince the film company first. Time enough to worry then, and there was always the chance that Zoe would lose interest — as she always did.

Zoe slid off the stool. 'Gotta go now, Mum, I need to wash my hair. I'll tell you all about it at Georgy's barbecue tomorrow.'

Georgy and her fellow school-teachers shared a house on the rural fringes of the city. The two females and a male were good friends and Kay always enjoyed a day in their company.

The big backyard was devoid of flower-beds, but a well-tended veg-etable patch flourished in a full-sun position. A large shady tree sheltered the barbecue area.

'How ever do you keep the grass under control, Georgy?' Kay asked. 'With a mob of sheep?'

'Isn't Wayne a treasure? That's why I insisted on the token male in the household. Your daughter is not just a pretty face.' Georgy laughed at herself.

Of the three sisters, she was the least blessed with conventional prettiness. She had inherited her maternal grand-mother's no-nonsense looks, but also Grandma's fine brain and love of children. Kay wished it was Georgy, not Zoe, talking of marriage — she deserved a good man.

Reminded, she asked her eldest daughter what she thought of Danny Quayle.

Georgy narrowed her eyes. 'Do you want my candid opinion?'

Kay nodded.

'I don't like him at all.'

Before Kay could ask why, there was an excited rush of people coming from the house. Zoe and the man they had been discussing led the way towards them, but, although he held a professional looking cam-corder on his shoulder, it was not Danny Quayle who commanded her attention.

Nor was it her daughters, Zoe and Alyce, or any of their friends.

Her astonished eyes had taken in the tall figure with them.

3

When she thought about it afterwards, Kay found it difficult to recall which of the mixed emotions that followed in quick succession affected her most. The unexpectedness of seeing Greg in the family situation was the first. She and her daughters had been a unit without a man for so long.

Bewilderment was next. Where had he come from? Who had asked him? And, more importantly, why wasn't she warned? She didn't have to wait for answers — Zoe was suddenly at her side.

'Danny and I met Dad at the airport because he had no idea where Georgy lived. It's cool, him being here, isn't it?' she bubbled.

Cool? Kay silently thanked her daughter for a reminder that it was what she needed to be now. If nothing else, her pride demanded it.

Zoe beamed at the man beside her. 'It was Danny's idea. Isn't he the most?'

The most what? Kay asked herself. The most presumptuous? The most inconsiderate? The most devious? What was his game? If he intended to win her approval he was going about it the wrong way.

Greg hadn't broken his stride, crossing the grassy space much as she'd seen him set off down the fairway in yesterday's televised golf tournament. It was clear success had given him a confidence that showed in his easy grace.

He reached her.

'Greg! What a . . . surprise!' she stammered, momentarily overcome.

'Kay,' was all he said, embracing her and kissing her first on one flushed cheek and then the other, in European style. There was a slight hesitation, as if he might add the more intimate third kiss, but decided against it.

At the touch of his lips, a sudden and

urgent desire, almost frightening in its intensity, gripped Kay. She wanted him back in their lives, and in particular, in her life. Just as suddenly came the knowledge that it wasn't possible, she had had her chance with Greg.

And had blown it.

Shaken, and afraid her face would betray her, she turned away from him and busied herself with preparations for the barbecue.

Soon, the sizzling of meat over charcoal competed with the voices and laughter on the summer air. It was a familiar and somewhat comforting sound that eased the tumult of her desires back to manageable levels.

She reminded herself she was a grown woman, not an impressionable girl like Zoe. She knew how to behave when confronted with an attractive male. Greg was an attractive male. And as Zoe said, it was cool.

Georgy came to stand beside her at the grill, edging her out of the way and at the same time, trying to take the barbecue tongs from her hand. 'Here, Mum, you go sit with Dad while we do this.'

Kay tightened her grip on the utensil, reluctant to give it up. Being face to face with Greg was what she wanted more than anything, and yet . . . she allowed herself a quick glance in his direction.

He stood chatting with Zoe and Danny at the other end of the trestle table. Then, as if he felt her inspection, he raised his eyes to meet hers. The capricious breeze changed direction and sent a cloud of tantalising smoke between them.

'Go on, I know he would like that,' insisted Georgy, then, as if understanding her mother's mixed emotions, added, 'You can do it.'

As she moved towards him, Kay wondered if there wasn't something of a conspiracy about this meeting. Had the girls planned this day, knowing Greg would be in the country for the upcoming tournament?

As she approached, Zoe and Danny found something else to do and disappeared, reinforcing her conspiracy theory.

'We're being relegated to onlooker status, Kay,' joked Greg as he organised two deckchairs and set them firmly on level ground. Turning back to the table, he gathered up two wine glasses and a bottle of wine before coming to stand beside her.

She wondered how he could act so calmly. Did that mean he knew nothing of what she suspected was their daughters' plotting? The brief glance she'd allowed herself showed a guileless face.

She was reassured, there was no reason for such a flight of fancy. He was in the country and the girls naturally wanted to see their father. What better opportunity than this?

There had never been any quarrel with him over access. From the start, Georgy had been old enough, and sensible enough, to take her sisters into the city to meet Greg on his infrequent visits to Australia. It had meant Kay didn't have to see him, her only contact being through their solicitor.

With hindsight, had that been a mistake? Could they have solved their differences back then? Kay shook off the thought, this was not the time for painful reminiscence and for what might have been.

'I don't suppose you're ever in a kitchen long enough to be bored, but I'm glad of the chance of letting someone else do the cooking,' she said, sinking into the nearest of the chairs.

'Is there cooking involved in your business?' he asked, filling their glasses and carefully standing the bottle on the grass beside the other chair, before sitting down. 'The girls don't say much about it.'

'Not a lot, actually. It's more light refreshments and gifts, chocolates, etcetera,' she replied.

'Successful?'

'Yes.' Even as she answered him, Kay

remembered. 'That is, it has been up until now, but . . . '

Greg leaned forward encouragingly.

'It's called progress,' she said, a note of bitterness she didn't intend creeping into her voice. 'There's always a developer wanting to cash in on backwaters like ours, almost as if they can't bear the thought of any corner of the country being left untouched, unspoilt.

'My argument is to leave something for those of us who value a more relaxed lifestyle and don't want a replica of a dozen other upmarket places around the bay. Somewhere with real trees instead of imported palms, and sand in your shoes instead of that other imported idea, a boardwalk, under your feet.'

Kay stopped, suddenly aware of her heated face and slightly raised voice. She took a quick gulp of her drink. This was not a suitable subject for a family barbecue lunch, it was too emotive.

Before she could think of another,

more acceptable topic of conversation, Zoe called, 'Is Mum on her hobby-horse again?'

There were laughs all round and under their cover Greg topped up her glass.

'Is the place under attack?' he asked lightly.

'Yes,' she answered, just as lightly. 'Don't mind me, it's been one of those weeks. But, tell me about yourself. As you said, the girls don't talk much about what's happening other than where it concerns them. All very normal.'

He nodded. 'Talking about the girls, it looks as if we're about to have our first wedding.'

Kay was not surprised he already knew. 'Zoe didn't waste any time. Did she let you out of the airport terminal before she told you?'

'As a matter of fact, Danny had been in touch with me a week ago, before I left the States, doing the proper thing.'

A week ago? Before they'd told her?

For some reason that hurt. Perhaps she was being unfair because she didn't like Danny. What could be more polite than asking the father of your intended bride for his permission?

Greg looked closely at her. 'Aren't you happy with this?'

Kay didn't know how to answer. This was their first face-to-face meeting in years and the conversation wasn't going the way she would have imagined, or wanted.

'It'll be a bit of a wrench, losing Zoe, I have to admit,' she answered. 'I don't know how I'll manage to live in a tidy house.'

'I heard that, Mum,' Zoe called.

'And it will be something of a thrill to take in the view from her bedroom window. I've almost forgotten what it looks like, but I seem to remember it was quite pleasant.' Kay leaned towards Greg, cupping a hand to her mouth. 'For years she's had a sign on the door warning of dire consequences to anyone who entered unlawfully,' she added in an exaggerated whisper.

'It's my only protection against Mum's vacuum cleaner,' protested Zoe, coming to stand beside Greg's chair and lay her hand affectionately on his shoulder.

'Very clever of you, Zoe,' remarked her father with mock-seriousness, tilting his head to look up into the face so like his own. 'Vacuum cleaners are the very devil.'

'Come and get it!' shouted Georgy across the laughter.

Before Kay could stir herself, Greg was on his feet. 'Let me get your lunch for you. A piece of steak, medium rare, with salad, no dressing. Oh, and horseradish, if there's any.'

Startled by him remembering her likes and dislikes, Kay could only nod. But why shouldn't he remember? There were many things about him that time and her determination had not been able to blot out. Did he still tug at his ear when puzzled she wondered.

She had recovered her voice by the

time he returned with two plates of food, and a bundle of cutlery wrapped in a napkin.

'This is something else, this being waited on,' she told Greg. 'I do appreciate it.'

He stood looking down at her, almost as if he was about to say something and then had changed his mind.

'What is it?' she asked.

He shook his head. 'It's nothing. Now's not the time.'

She knew better than to press for an answer, she remembered it was impossible to wheedle anything out of him until he was ready.

Lunch over, Zoe organised a game of backyard cricket, but despite her efforts, was unable to persuade Danny to take part. He circled for a while, at first training his camcorder on the group, then, as Zoe stepped up to the crease, concentrated solely on her.

New rules were invented as each player felt the need, which was often when caught leg-before-wicket, but there was no argument about the winner.

'I win! I win!' Zoe shouted exuberantly. 'I got the most runs.'

'That's because you're the youngest,' a breathless Greg reminded her, dropping on to the grass to lie on his back gazing skywards. Kay resisted the temptation to join him.

'This is the life,' he said to no-one in particular. Not sure she was meant to hear, Kay could only silently agree. It had been that kind of a day.

The sun was throwing long shadows across the yard before the group showed any sign of breaking up. Danny was the first to make a move, politely, but firmly organising their departure.

As Kay expected, he was the perfect guest, farewelling Georgy, his hostess, and then, in turn, each of the other guests, his left arm keeping Zoe at his side. The exuberant cricketer was gone and in her place, the well-behaved adult. Doing Danny's bidding, a little voice inside Kay's head niggled.

She knew she should be glad at this sign of maturity, but she wasn't.

She became aware that Greg had come to stand behind her, as, with a last wave, the young couple disappeared around the corner of the house.

'Don't be sad, Kay. She's growing up,' he murmured for her ears only.

In a rush of emotion, triggered by his empathy, she swung round to face him. 'But I don't want her to change!' she exclaimed. 'Not into that . . . '

'Is that your only reason?'

The group had broken up and moved off, cheerfully busying themselves with clearing away the remains of the barbecue. That left just the two of them, standing together in the last of the sunlight.

Kay searched his face, perilously close to confiding her fears. She wanted to tell him it wasn't so much about Zoe growing up as Danny's influence on their youngest daughter. How he seemed to control her.

She wanted to confess her doubts

about the unsuitability of the match. More than anything, she wanted to confess she didn't like Danny Quayle.

But even as the impulse was born, she thought better of it, afraid Greg might misunderstand, might suspect her motives, she had begun to doubt them herself.

Instead, she turned his question back on him and asked, 'You're not worried?'

'Should I be?'

She had no answer to that, either, at least not one she could give with any certainty.

Kay turned her head to watch the sun sink below the horizon in a blaze of colour. With it went the warmth of the day. She sighed, their lovely get-together was over. As the silence between them lengthened with the shadows she wondered if she would see Greg again before he left.

At last, he spoke.

'Kay, I was going to ask earlier if I might have a ride back to the city with you?'

Kay turned quickly to look at Greg, her eyes forced wide with surprise. Their day together was not over yet! Had he known what she was thinking? Just as quickly she lowered her gaze to hide her pleasure.

In the moment of hesitation before she replied, Greg hastened to reassure her. 'I can just as easily get a taxi if it's not suitable.'

'No, no, of course, it's suitable. I have an empty car and I'm going that way.'

4

The three men in business suits drained their coffee cups, pushed them aside and looked at Kay.

'Well then, can we rely on your support?' asked the spokesperson, the president of the Retail Traders' Association.

'Most definitely,' she replied.

'Excellent. We'll have three petitions to the Council going simultaneously, one here, one at the news agency around the corner and one at the post office. That should cover most of the residents.

'I'll get on to it immediately and send the forms and a clipboard over to you before lunch or soon after. We'll nip this tavern business in the bud before it goes any further.'

There was a chorus of agreement and a scraping of chairs as the group concluded their visit.

'You've got a good little business here, Kay,' remarked one of them, the owner of the menswear shop. 'You wouldn't want the tavern to take away any of your trade, would you?'

Kay was quick to put him right. 'It's not about that, Wayne, it's about changing the character of the area,' she protested. 'It's about traffic and parking problems, about the undesirability of serving liquor opposite a children's playground — '

'Yes, yes, all those things,' interrupted the president, obviously anxious to be getting back to his video outlet.

As promised, the petition arrived in the early afternoon. It attracted a good deal of notice from the start and the number of signatures soon grew. Kay was feeling quite upbeat about the chances of people-power defeating the proposed development.

'Well, I'll be off then,' said Ellen, late in the day. 'See you tomorrow.'

Kay looked up from checking her

accounts and glanced around the immaculate kitchen. 'It looks great, Ellen,' she said and bent her head to the task again. 'Put on the early-warning system as you go past, please,' she called as an afterthought

That amused Ellen. 'The early-warning system,' she repeated. Kay could hear her laughing as she left the shop.

It wasn't long before the soft tones of the electronic door-chime interrupted her. She stepped out of the kitchen. The last-minute customer, for the moment darkly silhouetted against the afternoon sun, was not a regular.

But he was not a stranger, either. 'Hello, Kay,' Greg said as he moved further inside, out of the glare.

Since the weekend barbecue, Kay had made a deliberate effort to keep thoughts of Greg out of her mind. There was no point in dwelling on the past and the what-might-have-been. Even the wonderful family day and their drive back to the city together had become the past, but in this case, not to be regretted.

As far as she knew, Zoe hadn't talked with her sisters since the barbecue so Kay's suspicions about a conspiracy between her daughters faded.

As Zoe became more involved in rehearsals, nothing was being said about her proposed wedding. Kay hoped that meant the romance was cooling.

'Greg! Whatever are you doing in this part of the world?' she asked, quite forgetting the golf courses nearby. Quickly she moved past him to lock the front door, turning over the *Closed* sign so that it faced outwards.

'Am I too late for a coffee?'

'No, the machine hasn't been switched off,' she replied, surprised at how calm she sounded. Quite different to how she felt. What would he think of her business venture? 'Take a seat. How do you like it?'

He looked around the tea-rooms, swivelling on one heel to take in first the shelves of chocolate closest the door, then the collection of tea-pots and cosies which gave the shop its name. He finally turned to face her across the serving counter. 'Very good,' he pronounced with a smile of approval.

'No, no, I mean, how do you like your coffee?' She could have added the words, these days, but stopped herself in time. 'At this time of the day.' She raised enquiring eyebrows.

'I'd like a long, strong black coffee, please,' he answered and chose a chair at the nearest table.

'Sounds like it's been a hard day,' she murmured as she served him.

'Not too bad really. My clients have all arrived and are out getting the feel of the course. I'm not needed just now.'

Intrigued, Kay asked, 'Are you their minder?'

He shook his head slightly. 'No, they bring their wives for that. I look after the business side of things, contracts, sponsorships, the press, all those matters.'

There was the tiniest of pauses. Kay rushed to fill it.

'Perhaps you'd care to sign our petition against the proposed tavern,' she suggested, reaching for the clipboard. 'But only if you believe a tavern would be a bad thing for around here.'

'I can see it means a lot to you, that's good enough for me.' He added a bold signature to the list of dissenters, but when he returned the clipboard she could see he had given his address as a city hotel.

Curiosity made her bold. 'You don't have a home address?'

He pocketed his gold-plated pen. 'You know the old saying, or was it a song, wherever I hang my hat is home? That's me. And talking of home, you'll be wanting to get there, if you've had a busy day.' He drank the last of his coffee and got up.

'I came by to ask would you care to join me tomorrow night at a function to mark the tournament opening? I realise it's during the working week for you, but it's also that for the golfers, so it won't be a late night . . . '

An invitation? It was the last thing Kay could've imagined. She got up, also, taking her time to carefully push the chair under the table so as to cover her confusion. And excitement. At last, she was able to look at Greg.

'Dinner?' she enquired, wondering what to wear.

'Yes,' he replied. Then, as if he could read her mind. 'Put on your dancing shoes, there'll be a little of that.' His eyes were dancing, too.

She responded to their challenge. 'Why not?'

'Am I to take that as a yes?'

She nodded, unable to think of anything else to say. 'Good. I'll come by at about six-thirty.'

Swept by surprising nervousness now she'd committed herself, Kay could only nod again and watch him go out the door.

A flash of undisguised admiration crossed Greg's face when Kay answered the door to him the next evening. She was pleased. It meant she looked her best.

She tried to pretend dinner with Greg was not a momentous occasion, excusing herself to Ellen when she took time off earlier in the day for a visit to the hairdressing salon.

It wasn't as if she'd gone overboard and bought a whole new wardrobe. She was wearing her reliable, go-anywhere little black dress, which she knew suited her. It was simple but elegant, a perfect foil to the rope of pearls and matching earrings. Strappy sandals completed the outfit that Greg saw.

And obviously liked.

What she hoped he couldn't guess at was the state of her inner self. Despite her efforts to remain calm, there was a heightened awareness of herself as a woman, which was missing whenever she went to dinner with David Brown.

* * *

The clubhouse at the Golf Club was buzzing. Although she lived not far away, Kay had never had occasion to visit it or any of the other clubs around the bay.

Despite numerous greetings, Greg didn't linger in the foyer. His hand at her elbow directed her determinedly through the crowd and into a glass-walled dining-room overlooking the course.

Kay and Greg were well into the evening, the conversation flowing easily between them, before Greg brought up the subject of their daughters.

'You've done a great job there, Kay,' he said.

'I don't like to claim too much credit. It's the old question, nature or nurture? Is it in the genes?' She smiled. 'They're good girls, all three did well at school, and Georgy and Alyce applied themselves at university. Now it's Zoe's turn,'

'Is that why you don't seem enthusiastic about Zoe marrying?'

Kay stared at him. She wished he hadn't asked her that. How much could she confide in him without seeming a controlling, even a manipulative, mother with her own agenda?

'I admit I was reluctant to agree to her taking this year off, having a gap year, if you like. But she wanted time to decide what she'd like to do. She had so many things she wanted to try. I had no idea getting married was one of those options. It came as a complete surprise.'

'Is that the only reason?'

'Why, hello.' The drawling voice saved her from having to answer. Greg's face changed, his brow furrowing at the interruption. If the man standing beside their table was at all sensitive to atmosphere, he could be in no doubt he was not particularly welcome.

'Hello, yourself, Damien,' Greg answered darkly.

Unabashed, Damien focused on Kay. 'Well, well this is a turn-up for the books. Greg Sheridan at a social function with a woman and a very attractive one at that.' He bent down, thrusting his face close to hers and becoming confidential. 'Greg is known as Garbo on the circuit, did he tell you that?'

Kay shook her head, fascinated by his brashness.

'That'll be enough, Damien,' growled Greg, but the man was not about to be brushed off.

'Do you know why?' he asked Kay. Without waiting for her answer, he straightened, threw his head back and struck a disdainful pose. 'I want to be alone,' he intoned with a thick accent.

The performance earned him applause from the group at the next table and cries of, 'Good onya, mate.'

'Aren't you going to introduce us, Greg?' Damien asked, without taking his eyes off Kay. Uninvited, he pulled up a spare chair and sat down.

'If you're thinking of becoming an actor I wouldn't give up my day job just yet,' Greg joked, accepting the inevitable with a return to good humour.

'Kay, you really wouldn't want to know this bad-mannered man, but his name is Damien Riley. Damien, this is Kay.'

Kay, she noted, not Kay Sheridan. It hadn't occurred to her that there would be awkwardness in introducing her. Legally, she and Greg were separated. Would anyone believe they had never filed for divorce?

Even as the thought crossed her mind, Damien Riley took her hand from where it lay on the table and grasped it warmly between both of his.

'Thank you for warning me,' she said to Greg, a little surprised, but entering into the spirit of the encounter. 'He certainly is, what my mother would call, forward.'

'And my mother would, too, bless her soul,' Damien interposed. 'Trouble is, I like what I see and faint heart never won a fair lady, you know.'

Kay's glance went from him back to Greg. She wasn't sure it was still a joke, one of this extrovert's party tricks. The people at the tables around them obviously knew Damien and were encouraging him from the sidelines.

His grip tightened, causing her rings to cut into her hand. She winced. He was quick to notice and turned over her hand to examine it.

'What have we here? A married woman, Greg?' Behind the banter Kay sensed a serious intent. She had no idea why it should matter to him.

She took the chance to withdraw from the man's grasp and hide both hands in her lap. Greg's face was inscrutable.

'Yes,' was all he said.

The onlookers, perhaps scenting the possibility of a confrontation, became silent, but nonetheless interested. Kay wondered what it was all about. Was there a long-standing dispute between the two men? Who was Damien Riley and what was he trying to prove? That he was brash and insensitive? He certainly was that.

Had he just had too much to drink? Why did the status of Greg's companion matter? Maybe, in the close-knit world of competitive golf it was accepted that everyone's business became everyone's. She couldn't know.

The small band struck up, Greg leaned across the table. 'I'm sorry about this, Kay. Would you like to dance?'

She nodded. And rose with him.

Greg looked down at the still-seated Damien, his face giving nothing away.

'I don't expect the mother, the excellent mother of my children, I might add, to have to listen to your drivel,' he said. 'Why don't you buzz off, Damien?'

Kay could feel his firm touch on her back as they threaded their way through the tables to the dance floor. She turned and slipped into Greg's arms with remembered ease, fitting her steps to his as if it was only yesterday that they had last danced together.

'Perhaps I shouldn't have told him that, should've just laughed it off as none of his business. He doesn't usually get under my skin,' he said above her head.

'Who is he?'

'He writes a newspaper column, mainly gossip about sporting people and events. Fairly harmless.'

'Do they really call you Garbo?'

He laughed, but said nothing, drawing her closer. The silence stretched as they circled the miniscule dance floor in perfect rhythm. It lasted until the music stopped.

He loosened his hold so that he could look into her face.

'Do you find Damien attractive?' he asked.

5

Kay laughed. She couldn't help herself, it was such an unexpected question. Greg obviously had no idea who or what had been on her mind as they danced and that was a good thing. It certainly hadn't been Damien Riley.

But, why was he asking? A flicker of purely feminine pride sprang into life. Was this jealousy? Or just masculine one-up-manship? Men were so competitive. Either way, it was a long time since she'd been the object of it, if she'd ever been.

Standing on the edge of the dance floor there was little time to search for reasons, Greg was waiting for an answer. She glanced over to their table — Damien Riley was still sitting there.

If Greg only knew, as far as she was concerned, there was no comparison between the two men. With a mild sense of panic she vowed he mustn't know.

'Why?' she asked lightly. 'Do many women find him attractive?'

'I'm asking you?'

'Is this a joke? A trick question?'

'No, it's just that he seems to have taken to you. I don't want to move him on if you like him.'

The warm feeling had flown. So much for feminine pride! There was only one answer.

'It's up to you, but I was thinking it was time to go,' she said. 'It's my busiest day tomorrow.'

* * *

Damien Riley stood at the counter, a small floral offering in his hand. He thrust it toward Kay with an ingratiating smile.

'I feel as if we have gotten off on the wrong foot at the golf tournament dinner-dance, and that drove you away. It was all in fun, I meant no offence.'

'None taken,' Kay answered. 'I have early starts during the week.' She looked down at the artistically-wrapped, potted cyclamen in her hand. 'Bought locally, I see. That's good. Won't you have something while you're here? Tea or coffee?'

'Thank you. Make it a cappuccino, please.'

'Take a seat, Damien. We seem to be quiet just now so I'll have one, too.'

By the time she joined him at the table with the two coffees, Damien Riley had already done a tour of the tea-rooms and was reading the petition against the proposed tavern. The pages of objectors' signatures had grown into a slim volume.

'Always the journalist, I see,' she remarked.

He put it aside. 'I'm not here as a journalist,' he said. 'Surely you know that. Question is, where do we go from here?'

Kay blinked with surprise. 'Go?'

She wondered if he guessed she wasn't used to such a direct approach or, for that matter, to many approaches at all. Married young, she'd had little experience in the flirting game.

The last few years of rearing the girls on her own and getting the business off the ground had meant there hadn't been many men to practice on. Like the place where she lived, her romantic life had been a backwater. By choice, she reminded herself.

'Life passes us by in Bayside,' she explained as an afterthought, to cover her astonishment. Greg had been right! Damien was interested in her.

The journalist was obviously smart enough to accept that she was flattered, but not at all receptive and changed the subject.

'I see the real world is beginning to catch up with you,' he commented, indicating the clipboard and the evidence of the community's protest.

'And we're not too happy about it, as you can guess,' she replied, reaching out to flip through the pages. Although relieved, she was a little piqued that he had given up the chase so easily.

'You could probably do with some publicity. It's not generally my field, but would you like me to bring a photographer down one day to do an article?'

'Oh, would you? That would be great.' Kay felt a friendliness developing between them. It gave her the courage to ask a question.

'Tell me, Damien, what did you mean about Greg being known as Greta Garbo on the golfing circuit? Why is that?'

'I would have thought it was obvious. He does an excellent job of looking after his clients' business interests but, apart from that, keeps pretty much to himself, socially. If you know what I mean.'

Kay nodded as if she did. He raised one eyebrow. 'You don't see much of him, do you?'

'You're amazingly perceptive, Mr Riley,' she said, drily, not wanting to admit anything.

'I'm a journalist, a good one.' He stood up. 'I take it that means there is no longer anything between you two. It's what I came to find out.'

Kay was dismayed. It had been a mistake to imagine he was ever anything but a journalist. Would he make something of it in his gossip column in tomorrow's newspaper?

'This is off the record, of course. For personal reasons only,' he reassured her as he prepared to leave. 'I'll be seeing you, then.' It sounded like a promise.

She stood for a moment, looking after him, her mind busy. Did he mean what he said? And could she trust him?

'There is something about a wedding in the family that brings out the romance in all of us, isn't there?' Ellen murmured as she passed, an order pad in her hand.

'Romance? Don't be silly,' Kay spluttered.

'We can use him in our campaign against the tavern, Ellen,' she explained later, under the cover of the hissing coffee machine.

'If you say so, Boss.'

★　★　★

Over the next week, the problems Kay had thought were pressing lost some of their urgency and were relegated to the back of her mind.

Days of glorious weather brought people out to walk along the foreshore and wander the shops. At the end of each day, footsore and weary, she thankfully closed the door on The Tea Cosy.

With the extra business, the increase in rent demanded by her landlord seemed manageable, and the petition against the proposed tavern was gaining more and more support.

Although she turned to Damien Riley's newspaper column with a touch of apprehension each morning, it made no mention of the relationship between Greg and herself. The journalist hadn't returned with a photographer, but she dismissed that as having been an empty promise, easily made and just as easily forgotten.

Kay did not see or hear anything of Greg, either.

She told herself this was a good thing, meeting him again had been unsettling. Even Zoe seemed happy, engrossed in her rehearsals, with no more talk of marriage.

It was the lull before the storm-in-a-teacup, Kay was to think later.

The place was crowded the afternoon Zoe excitedly burst through the door. Behind her was Danny and behind him trailed a gaggle of strangers carrying, among other things, a movie camera and sound equipment. They filled the shop, fanning out between the tables, jockeying to find a place for their particular requirements.

'We got it!' Zoe shouted, without regard for the startled customers.

'Got what?' asked Kay into the microphone that was suddenly thrust into her face.

'Oh, Mum,' laughed Zoe. For the camera, Kay realised with a sinking feeling. 'Danny has sold his idea to a production company. The wedding is going to be on television.' She embraced her mother. Again, for the camera.

The camera! With an effort, Kay overcame the automatic desire to reach up and smooth down her hair. She summoned a smile.

An interviewer was asking questions of the mother of the bride-to-be.

Somehow, Kay answered them and, after a last sweep of the café and its delighted patrons, the camera was switched off. It was only then that she allowed herself to look at Danny Quayle.

She didn't know what to make of the smile on her future son-in-law's face.

★   ★   ★

From that day on, it seemed to Kay that the movie camera ruled, intruding into their lives at every turn. Even the family dinner that night to celebrate Danny and Zoe's success became an opportunity for filming.

Nameless, bossy organisers from the TV production team made decisions as to where each person would be seated for the best camera angles.

Make-up artists leaned into the group, dabbing at each shiny face in turn, tweaking hair, then disappearing out of camera range. Kay found it hard to act naturally.

Zoe revelled in the attention, chatting animatedly about wedding plans, both with her fiancé and her sisters. The camera and microphone hardly seemed to worry Georgy or Alyce either.

Of course, Greg was also at ease, interaction with the media being part of his life with the golfing greats.

Kay wondered was she the only one with a sense of apprehension? Did all mothers-of-the-bride feel this way as the wedding juggernaut gathered speed?

Several times during the evening she caught Greg looking across at her.

When the camera and the blinding lights were finally turned off and just the family remained at the table, he came to stand beside her.

'Are you all right, Kay?' he asked.

She nodded. It wasn't the time or the place to voice her concerns.

He pulled up a chair and sat down. 'Does the camera bother you? You never did like the limelight, did you?'

Kay wanted to protest that she was over that, but knew it would only draw her into an explanation of her real disquiet about the wedding. Her dislike of media publicity, so necessary in his job, had been one of the stumbling blocks to her acceptance of his chosen career.

'I wonder if she knows what she's doing?' was all she said.

'She seems happy,' Greg said, looking across at their daughter and her chosen partner. He turned back to Kay. His eyes narrowed and became speculative. It made her uneasy.

'Why do I get the impression you're

against Zoe's wedding? Is it this particular marriage or marriage in general?' He lifted a quizzical eyebrow. 'You don't strike me as a bitter and twisted woman.' He reached out and touched her hand. 'On the contrary, you're a warm and caring person.'

As a blush of pleasure coloured her cheeks, Kay was glad the camera was no longer on them.

'It's all part of the deal,' said Zoe when Kay expressed her motherly concern over breakfast the next morning.

'Well, I'd like to know what the deal is,' she said. 'What does it involve? Why are your family being filmed?'

'Come on, Mum, lighten up.'

'Did they need to know you had a family?'

Kay knew it was a ridiculous thing to say, but events were moving too quickly and an open-ended commitment to be filmed was making her nervous. Did she want her quiet life exposed this way?

'You were all on the video Danny

submitted to the production company. Probably helped us win.' Zoe grinned. 'We're not a bad looking lot, as families go.'

'Video?' Kay remembered Danny filming the barbecue at Georgy's, the only time they'd all been together. The camera most likely captured the look on her face when Greg appeared.

She knew it would show more than surprise. Was it too much to hope that scene would end up on the cutting-room floor and Greg wouldn't see it?

'That was sneaky of you, Zoe. Did you think to ask whether we wanted to be involved?' she asked.

The smile was gone from Zoe's face. 'Why shouldn't you? You're family.' Tears filled her eyes. 'Don't you want me to be happy?' she demanded thickly.

Dismayed, Kay rounded the breakfast bar and threw her arms around her daughter. 'Yes, yes, I do, more than anything,' she exclaimed. 'I just wish I knew more about what is going on.'

Zoe untangled herself from her

mother's embrace, wiped away her tears with the back of her hand, and, with an exaggerated sigh, patiently began to explain.

'What we've got is the full cost of the wedding of our choice.'

'And?'

'And what?'

'What do the television people get in return for their money?'

'They film the preparations. And the wedding, of course. A sort of documentary, to be shown later in the year.'

Kay supposed there was some consolation in the fact that it wasn't going live-to-air, but inevitably, the worse-case scenario presented itself. How could she voice her fears without Zoe making fresh accusations?

'Is there an escape clause?'

Zoe frowned. 'What do you mean, an escape clause?'

Kay didn't answer. She couldn't remind her daughter of the many enthusiasms that had been hatched in this very kitchen, and subsequently become forgotten history. She couldn't do it.

She busied herself stacking the dish-washer and clearing the bench of the remains of their breakfast.

'I told Dad the TV people expect the father-of-the bride to be around for filming,' Zoe began in a more cheerful voice. 'So he's going to stay on in Australia until then. Isn't that great?'

The carton of milk slipped from Kay's nerveless fingers. It hit the bottom rack of the open refrigerator door and erupted in a white geyser down the front of the work outfit and on to the kitchen floor.

Aghast, Kay stood for a moment looking at the mess. Of course, weddings needed the father-of-the-bride and Greg staying on for that shouldn't have been such a surprise but somehow, it was.

She wondered if there were to be any more surprises.

There was one — Zoe took over. 'You go and change, Mum,' her daughter ordered. By the time Kay came downstairs, the kitchen had been restored to its pristine state. Most uncharacteristically.

Now that she was used to the idea, she had to admit Danny Quayle seemed to be good for her daughter, and having Greg around in the lead-up to the wedding would make things a lot easier.

Now that she was used to the idea.

'Thanks for cleaning up, Zoe. I don't know how it happened.' She gathered up her bag and car keys. 'Ready to go?'

Zoe nodded and followed Kay to the garage. Nothing was said between them until the last roundabout, when Zoe turned to her mother.

'You will say yes to whatever Dad asks, won't you, Mum?' she beseeched.

Kay's pulse quickened. She wished Zoe wouldn't spring surprises in the car; it always affected her driving.

'What do you mean?' she asked, warily, tightening her hands on the steering wheel.

'I can't tell you, but promise me

you'll say yes,' Zoe pleaded.

'It's impossible to promise that when I don't know what he's going to ask,' she replied in a pleasant voice. 'Just give me a hint.'

Zoe looked stubborn, and changed the subject. 'Could you let me out at the next corner, please, Mum?' I have to get some . . . something.'

Kay smiled as she pulled into the first vacant parking space she could find. Zoe was so transparent!

★ ★ ★

There was nothing unusual about the arrival of the two police officers during the morning. Officers often took a coffee break in the tea-rooms. It was part of their policy of a visible presence in the communities around the bay.

'Could we speak with you privately? The kitchen, perhaps?' asked the more senior man.

Kay stood aside, waved them through the bead curtain and followed.

'Could we see your list of people protesting against the proposed tavern, please?'

Kay relaxed with a laugh. 'Oh, thank goodness. I thought it was something serious. But why would you want to see that? It's a Council matter.'

The officer did not return her smile. 'This is a police matter,' he replied. 'Would you get it, please.' It sounded like an order.

They both followed her back into the shop. 'It's here beside the register, where everybody can see it. And hopefully, sign it.'

The petition was not there. 'Perhaps a customer has taken it to a table,' she suggested. 'Or left it on the shelf underneath one of the glass-topped tables.'

'Or it somehow got mixed up with the morning papers,' Ellen added, sorting through the rack before being called away by a customer.

Kay began to feel silly with the two police officers watching the fruitless search. It gave the impression of dithering and wasn't an image she felt happy with. She was a successful and efficient business-woman.

Back in the kitchen, she had to admit defeat. 'I'm sorry, it seems to have gone.'

Both officers nodded. 'We thought that might be so,' the spokesman said.

'What are you saying?'

'Can you remember when you last saw the petition?'

Kay had some difficulty remembering exactly. 'It's been there for a while and had become part of the furniture,' she laughed, then, when the officers remained unresponsive, quickly became serious again. She made a wild guess. 'I think it might have been yesterday afternoon . . . or the day before.'

'Did you notice anything untoward?' Kay and Ellen both shook their heads. 'Any strangers in the village? Anyone who showed an interest in the petition?'

'Any strangers?' That made Ellen laugh. 'The whole week has been full of strangers. The beautiful weather brought them flocking to the seaside,' she answered for Kay. 'We've been so busy . . . '

Kay's mind was busy, too. The last person, other than a local, who had shown an interest in the petition had been Damien Riley! Surely he wouldn't have taken it. And that was a week ago. She would've noticed it missing in that time. No, it couldn't have been him.

The policeman persisted with his questioning. 'Do you have any surveillance cameras?'

Cameras in tea-rooms? The idea was so ridiculous Kay looked at him for a sign he was joking. There was none. She shook her head.

'Pity. It might have helped us with our enquiries. There are only three businesses in the village collecting signatures. Both the post office and the news agency have reported their petitions missing, and now yours.

'We don't think all three of you could have been careless.' He gave her a wintry smile. 'And because all three are missing, we have to rule out random vandalism.'

He paused for effect.

'So, we have to assume they have been stolen.'

6

Stolen? Who would want to steal a petition?' Even as the policeman's eyes slid away from hers, Kay knew the answer to her question. If it wasn't vandals or the journalist, Damien Riley, there was only one other person who could be interested in the names and addresses of the people ranged against him and his proposed tavern.

Had the developers been one of the many strangers enjoying the burst of warm, seaside weather during the past week? It would have been easy enough to take advantage of the increased comings and goings to whisk away the petitions, under cover of a newspaper, perhaps.

But what could he do with the lists? Intimidate those who had signed? Kay looked out through the bead curtain to the pleasant room beyond and felt a twinge of guilt.

Her customers had been willing to add their names and addresses to the petition; she should have taken more care of that information.

She turned to the officers with a plea. 'Could we keep this quiet? I don't think my clientele would be happy if they were aware someone wanted to know who they were and where they lived. Especially not the older ones living alone . . . '

For the first time since the interviewing began both the policemen's attitude softened. The more senior of them answered. 'The post office has surveillance cameras that may or may not throw some light on what happened to their petition. The tape has been sent to headquarters to be examined. It will be Monday afternoon or Tuesday morning before we can expect a result.'

He parted the curtain and held it back for his colleague. 'Don't worry. I'm willing to bet the same perpetrator took all three petitions,' he said with a reassuring smile.

The perpetrator? Kay wondered if they had an idea of who that was. Did they share her suspicions?

'It's easy for him to say, don't worry,' she remarked to Ellen after the policemen had gone. 'What if the developer starts intimidating people?'

'How do you think he'd do that? It's impossible. Remember, we're not talking about a handful. Almost everyone in Bayside is against the proposal and must've signed one or the other of the lists.'

Kay realised Ellen was talking sense. Even with the lists there wasn't much the developer, whoever he was, could do.

When she was entering the takings on the computer at the end of the day, Kay found a clue to the developer's strategy. The closing date for lodging objections was marked on the wall calendar in front of her.

It was two days away!

She had to admit the timing of the robberies was clever. It was Friday night and replacement of the stolen lists of signatories by Monday was impossible. In the absence of any petitions to the Council, the developer could claim there were no dissenters to his proposal!

And have it passed.

It was hard not to feel defeated. An unspoilt environment, the cause so dear to her heart, seemed lost, Kay fought off the wave of despair that threatened to engulf her.

She had to. That night there was a cause even closer to her heart and she was determined nothing would spoil that. It was the long-awaited opening of Danny's production of South Pacific, and she intended to enjoy every moment of her daughter's stage debut.

★ ★ ★

The house was quiet when she reached it. Zoe had gone off cheerfully to the dress rehearsal the night before, followed by the camera crew, of course.

She stayed overnight with a member of the cast to be closer to the theatre.

Kay filled the bath and sank into its comforting depths, letting her whole body relax in the hot, scented water.

A new kind of nervousness took over as she dressed. She wondered if Zoe was suffering butterflies in the stomach, too, but for a different reason.

Kay couldn't fool herself it was only concern for her daughter making her hands tremble as she held up against her face this year's birthday gift from the girls.

At the time she'd thought the pendant earrings rather too showy, but now the cluster of beads and stones seemed ideal for the occasion.

The sound of the doorbell did nothing to calm her nerves. After one last anxious look at herself, she hurried downstairs and opened the front door to Greg.

'Are you sure you aren't the star, Kay?' he asked, almost as if he'd known what she'd been thinking.

'Not just the mother-of-the-star?' she prompted, a little breathlessly, she noticed. How could running down the stairs have affected her breathing? 'Come on in. Would you like a glass of wine or will we save ourselves for the back-stage party afterwards?'

'I'd prefer a coffee, if you wouldn't mind. We have time before we meet Alyce and Georgy.'

He followed her into the kitchen and looked around as she reached for mugs and the tin of shortbread. 'This always was a pleasant room, but what you've done is make it even better. Most welcoming.'

Kay kept her back to him for as long as she could, afraid to show her face. It wouldn't do for Greg to know how much his opinion mattered to her.

The camera crew waited for them at the entrance to the theatre. Greg took her hand and threaded it through to lie along his forearm, and held it there. As a couple, flanked by their two daughters, they stepped into the crowded foyer, and followed the cameraman.

It was Kay's first time at the centre of attention in public and she was glad of the solid reassurance of Greg's presence. And sorry when they were shown to their seats and he took his hand away.

Any fears she may have had for Zoe disappeared when the overture of well-loved music ended and the curtain went up on a South Pacific island.

The leading lady was no longer her youngest daughter, with her flyaway hair pulled back from her face into a ponytail, she'd become the older, but probably no much wiser, Nellie Forbush from Little Rock, Arkansas.

Impulsively, Kay turned to Greg. 'It's Zoe,' she whispered in delight.

He just nodded but the look on his face said it all — he was proud of his daughter, too.

Kay sat entranced as the story of the young nurse falling in love with the older, sophisticated planter unfolded. It was only when the most famous of the musical's songs ended with his advice to Nellie that the spell was broken and real life intruded. Once you have found your true love, never let them go!

The song touched a raw nerve that time had never healed.

Years ago, she and Greg had found each other across a crowded room, but she had let him go. It was not something she needed to be reminded of, especially not with Greg sitting beside her.

To her dismay, unwanted salty tears of regret welled up, obscuring her view of the stage. Desperately, she blinked to clear her eyes. The teardrops trembled for a moment on her eyelashes, then spilled over to slide silently down her cheeks.

Kay turned her head away and fumbled for her evening bag, hoping she'd remembered to put in a handkerchief when she was nervously dressing. And hoping she could dab at the tears without Greg noticing.

She was out of luck. Her fingers encountered some money, the house keys, a lipstick and a small comb. No handkerchief.

The tears, joined by others, rolled on down her face. She put up a hand to cup her chin in what she hoped was a natural gesture, thinking to flick them away casually. It didn't work — unstoppable, they seeped through her fingers and spread. Kay dropped her hand into her lap, praying Greg wouldn't look her way until the warmth of the theatre dried her shiny face.

Beside her, she felt him move, and a large handkerchief was pressed into her wet hand. She took it gladly, hid her face in it, and gave up the pretence that she wasn't crying.

'You're still a romantic,' Greg remarked as they made their way backstage for the party. She turned her head sharply to look at him, but there was no hint of ridicule in his face or voice. In fact, it sounded as if he considered that was a good thing.

Kay didn't know how to answer, other than promise to return his handkerchief. She had needed it again when the cast came out for their curtain call and received a standing ovation. That time they were tears of joy.

She had to admit Danny's revival of South Pacific had been a resounding success. The crowd of excited well-wishers that overflowed from the dressing rooms on to the stage were full of praise.

'Mum! Dad!' called Zoe above the hub-bub and pushed her way through. 'Did you like it?'

'Like it? Darling, it was wonderful and you were very, very good,' Kay exclaimed, wrapping her arms around Zoe.

'It was so good your mother cried, which is recommendation in itself,' said Greg, waiting his turn to hug his daughter. 'Where's Danny? I want to congratulate him.' He moved away.

'Mum, remember you promised to say yes to anything Dad suggests,' Zoe whispered urgently as soon as he was out of earshot.

'I didn't promise any such thing . . .' protested Kay.

The camera crew, complete with their bright arc light and microphone, surrounded them. It was time to record another family occasion. Not for the first time, Kay found the filming tiresome, she wanted to enjoy the evening with her family.

7

The film crew are likeable enough, but they do pop up in the most unexpected places,' she confided to Georgy who had materialised out of the crowd. 'We can't move without them. I'm afraid they'll film me in some embarrassing act, like with my mouth wide open catching flies.'

'Hang in there, Mum,' replied her daughter. 'The worst is yet to come. Imagine the three of us choosing our wedding outfits in the one room with the camera crew!' She began laughing. 'Hey, you should see your face! Watch out, the cameras!'

'Where? Where?' Kay asked, swivelling her head around wildly.

'Just a joke, Mum. Come in, let's join the others for the happy-snaps.' Georgy's laughter was infectious and soon Kay was laughing, too.

But the mention of the wedding sent her thoughts off in another direction. She had been counting the days to the opening night, expecting there would be a short run after that and the show would close. And Danny Quayle would depart. Without Zoe.

That night had come. But now Georgy was talking wedding as if it would go ahead. Did she know something?

It was in the early hours of the morning before Kay remembered Zoe's strange request. The family and a few friends lingered over the remains of supper and showed no sign of leaving the still-crowded restaurant.

Well-wishers were coming and going at the table and in the latest reshuffle, a chair beside her became vacant. Almost as if he had been waiting his chance, Greg moved swiftly to take it.

After calling for fresh coffee for them both, he settled down to talk to her. And satisfy her curiosity, she hoped.

Knowing their daughter, Kay imagined Zoe most likely planned on using

Greg to overcome maternal disapproval of her latest request, her own car as a wedding present.

'How are you going with your petition against the building of a tavern?' he asked.

She gave him a blank look. The tavern? She'd completely forgotten all about the police visit that afternoon. Whatever Kay had expected, it wasn't this.

'It's not good news,' she answered, remembrance temporarily clouding her evening of happiness. She proceeded to tell Greg what had happened.

'Everyone in the village is against it and now the three petitions have disappeared,' she added.

'What are you going to do?'

'What can we do? There isn't time to organise new lists before the closing time on Monday. I'm thinking of finding where the developer lives tomorrow . . . '

She glanced at the dainty dress-watch on her wrist and corrected herself. 'No,

I mean today, and letting him have a piece of my mind!' Indignation gave her voice an edge.

'Hey, whoa! You can't do that. If he's as smart as all this, he'd have you in court before you can turn around, for slander of defamation, or invasion of his privacy, or trespass. Any one of those. Take your pick.'

Although Greg sounded as if he was joking, Kay sensed there was more than a hint of seriousness in his advice.

'Thanks for cheering me up,' she said, drily.

Greg laughed at that, his eyes disappearing in a welter of crinkles. 'It's called taking an interest. It wouldn't do for the mother-of-the-bride to be in court on a charge, would it?'

Kay didn't feel able to laugh with him, she wished she could, but he'd brought up the matter of the wedding, guaranteed to reactivate her concerns. If she let it.

She made an effort to lighten up. 'I'd say that's called raining on my parade,' she joked. 'And may I remind you, the father-of-the-bride is supposed to support the bride's mother, not laugh at her.'

With an unexpected change of mood, Greg became serious. 'You're quite right.' He leaned towards her. 'That's something I've been wanting to talk about with you, Kay.'

8

The background noise of the party seemed to fade in that moment, leaving them in an oasis of quietness. Kay looked expectantly at the handsome face so close to hers, aware of the faint throb of a pulse at the base of her throat.

'Don't tell me, Zoe wants you to persuade me to agree to her own car as a wedding present,' she joked in a voice made high and light by excitement.

Greg was momentarily disconcerted by her answer. 'Er, yes, as a matter of fact, she does want a car.' He smiled. 'She's pretty persistent.'

Kay smiled back at him. 'Tell me about it,' she quipped. 'I call it her dripping-tap technique.'

They shared the parental moment, then the smile on his face faded, and his gaze wandered. 'But, that is not what I want to talk to you about,' he said over her head.

There was a long silence. Kay was puzzled. Greg's easy manner seemed to have deserted him and left him at a loss for words. It was unusual. What was it he found so difficult to talk to her about? She decided to help him.

'Is it about the wedding?'

It was the right thing to say. He brought his gaze back to her and almost eagerly seized the opening she gave him. 'I'm concerned about you having to do it all on your own.'

'But I don't have to. Most of the arrangements are being made by the film company.' And Danny, she could have added, but knew that it wasn't the time to bring up her doubts about their future son-in-law.

'The mother-of-the-bride needs support from the father-of-the-bride . . . moral support,' Greg went on.

Kay's heart contracted. What was he trying to tell her? That he was leaving? Was this to be an apology for running out on her? No wonder he was finding it difficult.

'That's true,' she admitted, sure he didn't know how much she needed him. The announcement of Danny and Zoe's wedding plans had only emphasised that.

The tightness in her chest moved down to become a hollow feeling in her stomach. 'But you'll be here, won't you? Zoe told me you were staying on in Australia until the wedding. Has that changed?'

'No, no,' he hastened to assure her. 'In fact, to give you that support I am wondering if it wouldn't be a good idea to move back home . . . into the house . . . with you and Zoe . . . until the wedding.'

Kay was almost giddy with relief — he wasn't leaving just yet. She wouldn't have to go through the lead-up to the wedding on her own.

It was a full moment before the practicalities of his suggestion hit her. Greg in the house! The thought of daily encounters knotted her already tormented stomach.

'If that wouldn't be too much of an intrusion,' he added.

An intrusion? Perhaps that wasn't the word to describe the effect his presence would have on the two-woman household. Yet, how could she refuse? It made good sense.

One part of her thrilled at the thought of seeing Greg every day until he left Australia again. Another was fearful that, in the intimacy of living together, it would be difficult to hide her feelings. And even more difficult to bear the pain when he left again.

In the end, it wasn't a hard decision. One of her mother's off-repeated sayings came to mind. Who will pay the piper? Of course, she'd willingly pay when the time came; it would be worth it.

Suddenly, something else occurred to Kay. It was all too coincidental. Her mind became fixated on the new possibility. What if this was a rather clumsy attempt, orchestrated by Zoe, to bring Greg and herself together? Would that make a difference? Kay knew it would.

Foolishly, she wanted to believe that it had been Greg's idea, not their daughter's. Disappointment swept her.

However unpalatable, she had to know the truth. Somehow, she found her voice. 'What about Zoe? How will she feel about . . . about your suggestion?'

'Zoe? I should imagine she'd be pleased,' he replied, looking across the restaurant in Zoe's direction.

Quickly, Kay pounced. 'Then she knows what you planned to ask me?' she demanded.

As if she had waited for a signal, their youngest daughter hurried over. Kay's suspicions deepened — it had to be a conspiracy.

'Mum, have you said yes?' Zoe asked. 'Am I to get my own car?'

A twinge of guilt shot through Kay. She'd been too quick to judge both Greg and Zoe.

'We haven't got around to discussing that yet, Zoe,' Greg replied, his eyes on Kay, one eyebrow raised, waiting for her to answer.

'Well, what have you two been talking about all this time?' Zoe demanded of them both.

Kay took a deep breath. 'Your father and I have decided it would . . . make sense for him to be in the house . . . for the wedding,' she said.

Greg had been right, Zoe was pleased. With a whoop, she embraced her father. 'Stay with us? Just wait until I tell Danny.' In a whirlwind she was gone.

'I told you she'd be pleased,' Greg laughed, watching their daughter's excited rush across the room before turning his attention back to Kay. Their eyes met. 'And I am, too, Kay.'

★   ★   ★

Kay sat at the breakfast bar, her hands wrapped around a mug of coffee. The empty house creaked as the morning sun reached and warmed it.

She was glad Greg wasn't coming until late in the afternoon. It gave her time to air his room and catch up with some chores before preparing a light meal for the three of them.

Last night's heightened state of nervousness had been replaced by a mood of pleasant anticipation; dreamily, she contemplated the garden through the open windows. The second flush of roses beckoned.

Taking up the secateurs and a basket as she passed, Kay moved out into the Sunday quiet. All around, the neighbourhood was peaceful, no roaring motor-mowers or heavy traffic disturbed its tranquillity.

She stopped short. Not yet! In the excitement of Zoe's stage debut, and Greg's astonishing request, she'd forgotten the threat that lay over their paradise. There must be something I can do, she agonised.

But what? Greg warned her against

taking on the developer and risking legal action. He was probably right, but she couldn't let that stop her. The trouble was, she didn't know where the developer lived.

The pleasure of the morning was gone. Feeling utterly frustrated, she went back inside the house and began to rather carelessly arrange the roses in a vase.

The sharp pain of a thorn piercing her finger and breaking off drew an involuntary exclamation from her lips. It did nothing to improve her mood.

Carefully, she removed the thorn and reached for a tissue to blot up the drops of blood welling up from the tiny puncture. Then, seeking a band-aid, she pulled out the kitchen drawer that held the first-aid kit.

On the top of its miscellaneous contents was Damien Riley's business card, slipped in there instead of into her office drawer. She couldn't remember doing it.

Kay seized on it, her bleeding finger

still wrapped in a tissue, the search for a Band-aid forgotten. As a journalist, Damien Riley had connections — they would know the developer!

It was as if fate had taken a hand. There was still time to do something about the proposed tavern! She dialled his mobile phone number.

'Who is it?' a sleep voice asked.

'Is that you, Damien?'

The answering grunt was not encouraging. Kay glanced at the clock. Perhaps she should apologise for the early call.

'It's Kay Sheridan. I'm sorry to be calling at this hour on a Sunday morning, but there isn't time to waste . . .'

'Kay!' There was nothing sleepy about the way he said her name — he sounded almost pleased.

She explained what she needed. And why.

'Can do. I'll get back to you,' he said.

9

She thought it would be in the form of a telephone call, but within an hour the doorbell rang. Damien Riley stood on the doorstep. He was not alone. His companion was weighed down by the camera and various lens cases and light meters that hung around his neck.

Kay drew back at the sight of him — she'd had enough of view-finders being trained on her. And certainly, if she was about to do something foolish, she didn't want it captured on film.

'How did you know where I lived?' she asked.

'We're bound to catch him at home before lunch on a Sunday,' Damien said conversationally, ignoring her question.

'But a photographer?'

'I promised you I'd get you some publicity. It seems I'm running a bit later with that, but there's bound to be a story in this. News is scarce on a Sunday.'

Kay looked beyond him to the car parked in the street. There were two men in the back seat, rather big men, she noted. Did Damien have it in his mind to make news? Too late, she remembered Greg's warning.

'Who are your friends, Damien?' she asked.

He gave her a wink. 'A couple of mates. They felt like a Sunday drive to the seaside.'

It all seemed too heavy-handed for Kay.

'Look, I only wanted to confront the developer and try and change his mind,' she explained. 'Not start a fight and get into trouble with the law.'

He shrugged his shoulders. 'So you've got cold feet, eh? Oh well . . . ' He gave the photographer a nod and both turned toward the car.

Dismayed, Kay called after him. 'Wait, Damien!'

It was only when he turned his

laughing face back to her that she realised he had been teasing.

'OK, we'll play by your rules, no fisticuffs. He'll probably crack at the sight of a camera, anyway,' he said. 'Come on, follow us!'

★　★　★

The two-car convoy travelled for an hour before reaching an affluent suburb of the city. The wide, leafy streets flanked by large houses reflected their owners' wealth.

Kay parked behind Damien as he pulled up near a set of imposing iron gates. Topped with dangerous spikes that obviously weren't for show, they sent a clear message — uninvited visitors not welcome! She doubted she'd get past them.

Her emotions were on a roller-coaster again. 'This is a mad idea,' she confessed to Damien, her dry mouth making it hard to form the words.

'Just keep your mind on the job,

and get us in,' he urged, pushing the intercom button for her and stepping away. 'His name is Michael Lewisham.'

The speaker-box crackled into life and a disembodied voice asked, 'Who is it?'

As she leaned forward to answer, the camera flashed. 'My name is Kay Sheridan,' she croaked. 'I want to talk to you about one of your proposed developments.'

The voice became wary. 'Which development?'

'The tavern at Bayside.'

There was a snort of amusement. 'Well, Mizz Sheridan, you're too late. There's nothing to talk about. The proposal goes before the Council tomorrow night and I can assure you, it's going to be passed.'

Michael Lewisham's almost gloating tone infuriated Kay. Any idea that she could talk reasonably to the developer, perhaps persuade him to locate his tavern elsewhere, was gone.

'That's what you think, Mr Lewisham,'

she shouted into the speaker-box. 'You've been caught on a surveillance camera stealing the petitions! The police are — '

There was a click and the intercom became silent. The developer had cut her off. And not before time, she realised.

'I can't believe I said that,' she gasped. 'I don't know that he's on the tapes, do I? He could — what could he do, Damien?'

There was an air of disappointment about the group, almost as though they'd been cheated out of something.

'Don't worry about it, Kay,' Damien replied, casually. His attention was on his photographer. He nodded. To Kay's astonishment, the man began scrambling up the ivy-clad wall.

'What's he doing, Damien?' she asked stupidly. It was obviously what the police would call trespassing.

Damien took her arm and propelled her toward her car. 'He's just getting background pictures,' he said, opening the driver's-side door for her. 'For the article,' he added, skirting behind the car to the passengers side.

'Why don't we go down to Acland Street for brunch?' Damien suggested. 'I haven't had breakfast.'

There was a thud and a grunt as the photographer landed on the other side of the wall. Seemingly unconcerned for his safety, the two silent men turned away and resumed their seats in Damien's car.

'What about your friends?' Kay asked, watching them uncertainly.

'They can look after themselves,' he said with a cheeky grin.

* * *

Kay took the turn into her driveway too fast, only just avoiding the car parked there. Greg was early! She had intended to be ready for his arrival, cool and in control, not like this, rushed and out of breath. And with a guilty conscience!

It was all Damien Riley's fault! Brunch with him began out of a sense of gratitude for his efforts and had gone on too long, she knew that, but he had been so entertaining.

Eager to put the morning's debacle behind her, she'd lapped up his flattery. And promised to meet him again! She groaned inwardly.

The familiar murmur of the television greeted her as she opened the door. It meant Zoe was home, too.

Father and daughter were seated on the couch in front of the set. The two dark-haired heads, identical in colour, turned to greet her as she stepped into the living-room.

'Where have you been?'

10

Only a young, beautiful, indulged but, much-loved daughter could be so blunt, thought Kay.

'I've been out,' she replied, biting back an automatic rebuke. But Zoe had already lost interest in the answer and turned her attention to the television screen again.

'It's the video of last night,' she enlightened her mother over one shoulder. 'We couldn't wait any longer for you.'

Conscious of Greg's eyes still on her, Kay moved through to the downstairs powder-room. Did she imagine he could see guilt written all over the flushed face that gazed back at her from the mirror?

She ran the cold-water tap and bent over the basin to splash water on her face until the heat went from it. And there was no longer any reason to hide.

Greg came into the kitchen as she began preparing a batch of scones.

'We've already played the video twice,' he said with a rueful smile. 'Even a doting father couldn't be expected to sit through it again.'

Looking completely at ease, he perched on one of the breakfast-bar stools. 'Georgy rang. She and Alyce are coming over. They'll have to see the video, won't they?'

'And so will I,' Kay smiled sympathetically. 'Do you have a good book you can read?'

'Don't laugh, there's more. I heard Zoe mention bridesmaids' dresses. Not exactly men's talk.'

'You and Danny will have to find something else to talk about,' she remarked above the clatter of putting together the ingredients for scone-making.

'Danny's not coming,' Greg said.

Kay's smile became genuine again. She was pleased, it meant she and the girls would have Greg to themselves for the evening. She enjoyed the thought for a moment then frowned, disturbed by another.

However was Danny to become a member of the family if he avoided family gatherings? The last time they'd all been together as a group had been the barbecue at Georgy's, weeks ago. At the beginning of the filming.

'Is it business again? On a Sunday?' She realised she was giving the dough a thorough work-out and stopped. Overkneading would make the scones heavy.

'What is it that is worrying you?' Greg asked.

His concerned tone opened a longing to confide in him, to express some of her doubts. But was this the time to share her fears for their youngest daughter? Zoe was in the next room, reliving her triumph, and Georgy and Alyce could arrive at any minute.

She closed the oven door and, with her answer ready, faced Greg. 'It's just that I'm a mother . . . Why are you looking at me like that? Isn't it normal to worry about your children?'

He didn't comment. Instead, he leaned across the breakfast-bar and brushed her cheek.

'Flour,' he said.

The unexpectedness of his touch unnerved Kay. She swung away and began noisily loading the dishwasher. What had she let herself in for? It was going to be hard having him in the house if she let every little thing do this to her. She mustn't, she determined.

Composed once more, she straightened up and checked the kitchen for any last minute additions to the load. 'Will you pass me . . . '

There was no need to ask, Greg had already stretched his arm out to reach the coffee mug left beside the phone when she rang Damien for the developer's address.

'It's not empty,' he warned as he lifted it. A business card clung to the bottom of the mug for a moment, then was dislodged. It fluttered to the floor and landed print-side up.

There was nothing discreet about Damien Riley's card, Kay could read the flamboyant lettering from where she stood.

Greg's eyes came back to her face, his own an inscrutable mask. He put the mug within her reach, bent to retrieve the card and lay it on the bench-top between them.

She wanted to explain but reminded herself she didn't have to say a thing.

*   *   *

Greg was in the living room when Kay came downstairs the next morning. He sat by the window in a patch of morning sun that highlighted something she hadn't noticed before, the first sprinkling of silver in the dark hair at his temple. It gave him a distinguished appearance.

'Good morning, Greg,' she called up on her way through. 'I didn't hear you get up.'

The tantalising smell of percolating coffee hung about the kitchen.

'Oh, and thank you for getting the coffee going. I'm definitely running behind time this morning.' She half-filled a mug and turned back toward him.

'You'll be pleased to hear the wedding dresses have been decided on. After all that discussion last night, which you sensibly avoided, it was surprisingly painless. All we need now is to match their ideas to availability.'

Without commenting, Greg got up from the chair and came from the other room, the newspaper still in his hand.

'There's a full-page article by your friend, Damien, in the paper this morning,' he said. 'With photographs.'

Kay felt a tiny clutch of apprehension — his face was unreadable. It hadn't always been that way; once she would have known exactly what he was thinking.

'Oh, what about?' she asked with a casualness she didn't feel, turning away to top-up her coffee mug.

'You should read it,' Greg replied, folding the newspaper and placing it on the breakfast bar so that the article was uppermost.

She was almost afraid to look. Was it too much to hope she wasn't mentioned? A quick glance recognised Damien's photo and by-line that headed the page, but nothing more.

'Later, Greg. I'll have to hurry if I'm to open on time. There are regulars who rely on me.' She thought fleetingly of David Brown. 'For my muffins.'

'How come Damien is writing about this place?'

'He promised us some publicity over the proposed development . . . ' she busied herself with plates and cutlery. 'Of course, it's come too late.' She glanced at the kitchen clock. 'I'll have to call Zoe. Will you look after your toast?' She waved a hand toward the bread and hurried away.

The morning at The Tea Cosy began slowly. Kay was glad, it gave her a chance to get her thoughts in order. After the delight of a family evening meal and the unfamiliar morning routine with an extra person in the house, she needed it.

When Zoe came to breakfast she seemed more subdued than usual. Kay guessed she was probably feeling flat after the build-up to her stage debut and the excitement of her success, that would be a normal enough reaction.

'She's not good in the morning,' Kay explained in an aside to Greg as they left.

The policemen arrived as the first batch of savoury muffins was cooling on the rack, the freshly-baked smell filling the, as yet, empty tea-rooms.

'You've timed your round perfectly,' she said, taking out her order-pad, expecting them to sit down.

'We're just passing,' the older of the two explained, without pulling out a chair.

Kay looked at him enquiringly. 'Isn't it too soon for a result from the surveillance camera?'

'There's been a development we . . . my mate and me, thought you should know about,' he replied carefully. 'Off the record,' he added, glancing at his partner for confirmation.

The younger man nodded, his attention wandering to the rack of muffins like a man who hadn't breakfasted.

Kay picked up on it. 'Are you sure you haven't time for something?' she asked. Her suggestion was ignored by the more senior officer.

'A person came into the station yesterday and returned a petition,' he said, breaking the awkward silence.

Kay felt a surge of relief. 'Then it's not too late for it to be presented at the Council meeting tonight!'

This time the officer did not hesitate, cutting in quickly to quash her hopes. 'I'm afraid that will not be possible. We will have to retain the petition as evidence.'

'But why would you want to do that? If the petition's back, isn't that an end to it?' Something about his manner made her wary. 'There has to be more. Whose petition is it?'

The policeman looked even more uncomfortable. 'I am not able to comment on the matter any further, not able to give you that information . . . ' He looked at his companion. 'Constable, perhaps you could go around the corner and inform the newsagent a petition has been returned to us and our enquiries are continuing.'

The younger man was not pleased. 'But I want — '

'If you hurry, the coffee will be ready when you get back.' It was almost an order.

Watching the clash of wills, Kay could hardly contain her rising impatience. This was not the time for personal stand-offs and pulling rank.

'Don't you understand? At least one petition has to go before the Council tonight, or it's too late,' she reminded them both. 'Why can't you do something?'

Neither policeman answered her, still staring each other down. At last, the younger man gave way, turned on his heels and disappeared out on to the street. There was an immediate change in the remaining man's manner. He turned to Kay.

'It's a matter for CID now,' he explained almost apologetically.

Police procedure and the formality of their language was beginning to annoy Kay. 'This is hopeless. We're no better off.' She threw up her hands in a gesture of futility. 'I'll get started on your order,' she said, turning toward the coffee machine.

'No, stay here,' he said, his glance straying to the door. 'The thing is, the person who returned the petition claims to have accidentally picked it up with his purchases. But, that is not possible.'

'Not possible?'

The policeman stood silent.

It took a full minute for Kay to get his meaning. She remembered each list was headed up by the name of the business and he was telling her the petition that had been returned didn't tie in with the person's story.

'But, as there is no surveillance camera either here or in the news agency, we can't actually question his statement? Is that what you're saying?'

'That is correct, as I understand it. No camera,' the officer repeated.

'He could claim forgetfulness, couldn't he? Say he was in both businesses that day. But how could anyone make such a mistake, pick up a petition that size with a gift-wrapped box of chocolates or a takeaway cup of coffee?'

The policeman stared at her, as if willing her to make sense of what he couldn't divulge.

'So, it still means, until we see the post office tapes, we have no way of proving if he is the perpetrator, or if what he says is correct or incorrect.'

She was getting as bad as the police with her formal language. 'I mean, is the truth. Are you sure you can't tell me who that person is?'

'I am not able to say any more,' he said, putting such emphasis on the first word she got the message.

'But I am?'

The slight movement of his shoulders could hardly be classed as a shrug. 'I am obliged to answer any question from the public not relating to pending charges.'

There was an awkward pause. Kay couldn't think of a thing to say that didn't come under that heading; to her, it was back to being a hopeless cause.

'Do you know anything about the liquor licencing laws?' the policeman asked at last. 'As I understand it,' he went on without waiting for an answer, 'a licence to sell liquor cannot be granted if the applicant is considered by the police to be an unsuitable person. Even a minor infringement of the law could be deemed a deterrent to approval.'

Something like hope flickered into life.

'Are you saying that if the . . . the person on the tape is shown to be Michael Lewisham — ' Kay broke off at the look on the officer's face. It was not encouraging. She had gone too far by naming names.

'Let me rephrase that. If it is shown to be the same person as the one who returned this petition, investigations could lead to a charge being laid and . . . ?'

The policeman nodded. 'That would be a likely outcome, if that were the case.'

Kay grinned. Without telling her, the officer had let her know who the suspect was — the developer, Michael Lewisham! Her visit and talk about tapes must have forced him into concocting a convincing story.

But being a stranger in the village, he had no idea which of the three businesses had surveillance cameras. And because she was making the accusations, had chosen the wrong one!

She felt a surge of victory that died

almost immediately.

'But what about the Council meeting tonight?' she asked. 'If we don't have even one petition to put to them . . . '

'I believe the Council will be advised there has been interference in the due process of their bylaws relating to objections to a proposal.' He allowed himself a ghost of a smile.

★ ★ ★

In the late afternoon Greg came into the tearooms. 'Do you have time for a talk?' he asked.

'Of course, Ellen is still working,' she answered, taking off her apron and joining him at a table. 'Oh, Greg, the most wonderful thing has happened! My missing petition has turned up and because there has been interference in the ratepayers' right to object, the Council will refuse to consider the application. And this is all without identification from the surveillance tapes — '

'Hey, slow down! Your friend, Damien, did this?'

For a moment, Kay didn't understand him. In the excitement of the policeman's information, she'd forgotten to read Damien's article. What had he written to give Greg this impression?

Was the journalist claiming he'd approached the developer? It was her idea. Indignation rose in her and brought her close to divulging details of their Sunday excursion. And her part in it.

She stopped herself in time. 'Sorry?'

'Do you find him attractive?' he asked in a low voice, almost as if he could no longer contain himself.

His words, thick with suspicion, were scarcely discernible above the murmur of the customers' conversation. Not sure that she'd heard him right, Kay stared at the tense face opposite her. Why did the journalist worry him so much?

'That's the second time you've asked me that.'

Her astonishment obviously embarrassed Greg. He quickly recovered his composure, and with an effort, tried to divert attention from what he'd said with a dismissive wave of his hand.

'I'm happy for you, but that's not what I came to talk to you about.' He looked about him. 'How do you access the rooms above?'

Kay couldn't follow the erratic conversation, 'The what?' she asked.

'This building obviously has a second storey. Is it included in your lease? If so, where are the stairs? Outside?'

Still quite bemused, Kay nodded. She led him out on to the street and unlocked a frosted-glass door next to the tea-rooms. It revealed a well-lit staircase between the two buildings.

'Ellen's due to finish now so I'll have to leave you to look by yourself,' she said, handing him a bunch of keys.

It wasn't long before Greg was back. He came into the kitchen looking pleased.

'If you're agreeable, I'd like to sub-let the main rooms upstairs.'

11

Kay stared at Greg, unable to get her head around what he was saying. The idea of putting the upstairs rooms to some use was not new, but he was the last person she would've thought as a tenant.

Why should he want to sub-let office space? To use as a store-room whenever he came back to Australia, perhaps? But, to store what? As she understood it, his work was with professional golfers, organising their careers, which could be managed by telephone and computer, and wouldn't involve merchandising.

And, if he became her tenant, it meant she would be seeing him whenever he came back to Australia. Was that what she wanted? It was a tempting scenario, but she had already conditioned herself to him going out of her life once the wedding was over.

Before she could ask any of the questions racing through her mind, the bell in the tea-rooms rang. Somehow she collected herself and attended to what she decided was to be the last customer for the day.

She followed the woman to the door, locked it after her and turned the *Closed* sign to the outside.

Greg had come from the kitchen. He pulled out a chair for her and held it until she sat down then joined her. Kay felt a faint tremor of excitement.

Hoping to hide her nervousness, she leaned her elbows on the table, her chin resting on her tightly-clasped hands, and looked to him for an explanation.

'I've decided to branch out into something different, and need a base to work from. These rooms are ideal for me and the extra money would solve your problems with your landlord,' he said.

Kay was feeling she'd missed something. How did he know about the landlord's demands for an increase in the rent? Had the girls told him?

'I'd thought of sub-letting, but . . .' she stammered. 'Yes, I have to admit that would be a great help financially. But, I don't understand . . . what are you going to do with the rooms?'

'I've decided to give up the travelling . . .'

Kay's hands tightened still further.

'Being home and involved with the girls . . . I have no desire to go back to that . . .' His voice trailed off.

There was a long silence.

An almost forgotten remark by her assistant came to Kay's mind. Weeks ago, Ellen had said weddings made everyone romantic. Was it too far-fetched to imagine that was happening between her and Greg? Had Zoe's approaching wedding been a catalyst?

Not for the first time, she wondered were their daughters working behind the scenes to bring their parents back together. She wanted to ask him, but didn't dare. After all, he hadn't mentioned her, only the girls.

'I intend to set myself up as a consultant,' he said at last. 'I'll need offices for that.'

Kay was glad she hadn't asked. This was clearly business, nothing to do with her. So much for your foolish notions of romance, she told herself wryly.

'I can see a future as an organiser of special events, golf days for the corporate section, charity tournaments, that sort of thing. I have the connections both here and overseas and the respect of the industry.' His face darkened. 'Hard-earned.'

Kay refused to let his reference to the past take her down the path of what-might-have-been. The new idea of Greg back in her life on a permanent and daily basis, even if only as a tenant, needed getting used to.

He waited for her response.

The handle of the locked front door rattled, followed by insistent rapping on the glass. Startled out of the moment, Kay turned. It was Zoe, pointing to her watch, her body alive with laughing impatience.

'Oh, is it that time already?' exclaimed Greg, getting to his feet. 'I promised her a ride home.' He briefly touched Kay's shoulder as he passed. 'We'll talk about this later.'

★　★　★

The smell of cooking teased Kay's nostrils the moment she opened the front door that evening. As she entered the living-room the animated chatter died.

Danny Quayle got up from the couch. She supposed he was there for the announcement of the wedding date, and looked around for his retinue of camera crew with their paraphernalia. They were nowhere to be seen. That seemed odd to her.

Surely setting the wedding day was a big moment in the filming.

'Whom do I have to thank for this?' she asked, sniffing the air appreciatively and waving a hand in the direction of the kitchen.

'Dad,' answered Zoe. 'He knows how to roast a leg of lamb and everything. But I did the vegetables and set the table.' There was an air of suppressed excitement about the bride-to-be.

'Greg?' exclaimed Kay.

Greg laughed and gave an exaggerated bow before pouring her a glass of wine. 'To new beginnings!' he proposed his toast encompassing each of them.

'New beginnings!' Zoe and Danny clinked glasses.

Kay did her best to respond to the light-hearted mood. 'New beginnings in the kitchen? I'll drink to that.' However short-lived, she could've added.

There was an exchange of glances between Danny and Zoe. Kay readied herself for the inevitable. Her fears that Danny Quayle would somehow break Zoe's heart had been unfounded.

Now she had to be big enough to admit she was mistaken and accept him into the family. She put on a smile.

'Zoe and I have decided to go our separate ways and not get married,' Danny said in his precise manner.

Unable to control her astonishment, Kay's hand shook, spilling some of the contents of her wine glass down the front of her clothes.

'You're not disappointed, are you, Mum?' Zoe asked when all the fuss had died down.

'Disappointed? I don't know. Surprised is more the word for it. You've put so much planning into the wedding.' Suddenly weak-kneed, Kay felt behind her for an easy chair. 'I need to sit down.'

12

This last surprise in a day of surprises had left her almost dizzy with happiness. First, the tavern proposal had been thwarted, at least for the time being, and, now that she was used to the idea, Greg's announcement that he was staying on in Australia would solve her financial concerns for The Tea Cosy.

Kay didn't really care why the wedding had been called off, just that it was and her wishes for her daughter's continued happiness had been fulfilled, seemingly without Zoe being hurt.

There was a fleeting moment of regret about the carefully-chosen dream wedding dress that hung behind the door of Zoe's room. Despite the presence of the film crew, she had enjoyed the evening spent in a city bridal salon with her three daughters.

'And the big news is — '

'Bigger than that?' Kay recovered enough to interrupt her daughter with an amused glance towards Greg, but Zoe was not listening.

'I've been offered a place as a drama student at the College of Performing Arts!' she announced. 'Danny arranged for the head of the selection panel to attend opening night of South Pacific and he thought I was good.'

'And so you were,' Kay said, getting up from her chair and hugging Zoe.

'I'm so excited,' said Zoe, breaking away from her mother to twirl around the room. 'It's what I've always wanted to do.'

Always wanted to do? Last month she had wanted to get married. Kay smiled to herself at the enthusiasm. That was one of the things about being young. Perhaps acting truly was to be Zoe's future life. Perhaps not.

Greg came to stand beside Kay and put an arm across her shoulder. She had forgotten how good that felt, how much she'd missed its reassurance.

'Whatever path you choose, you take our love with you, Zoe,' he said for both of them, reaching out the other arm to bring their daughter into a hug.

Tears welled in Kay's eyes. He couldn't have put it better, she only wished for happiness for each of her girls, and she knew Greg felt the same.

Over his shoulder, Kay became aware of Danny standing outside the family circle. Although she had not liked him from their first meeting, she had no desire to hurt him. He had behaved impeccably.

Their eyes met. 'Thank you,' she mouthed, hoping he would understand. He did. His face softened for an instant before he nodded imperceptibly. Touched, Kay wondered if the decision not to marry was entirely mutual.

'And what plans do you have, Danny?' she asked, detaching herself from the embrace.

For once, Zoe answered for him. 'Danny is going into film production.'

'Not before he tastes my roast leg of lamb with rosemary potatoes, I hope,' joked Greg, slapping him on the back. 'Come along, everyone, it's dinner time.'

★ ★ ★

Kay stood at the french windows, aware she was happier than she'd been for some time. Behind her, the dishwasher hummed in the darkened kitchen, the comforting domestic sound a backdrop to the distant crash of the incoming tide.

The rising wind that carried with it the strong smell of seaweed caught a neighbour's unlatched gate and banged it shut.

'There's a change coming,' she remarked, closing out the night and turning to Greg with a smile. 'And I mean in the weather, not in our lives. That's happened already, hasn't it?'

He leaned forward and took up the percolator from the tray on the low table. He poured coffee for them both then patted the couch beside him.

'You weren't terribly disappointed that the wedding has been called off, were you? I know you thought Zoe was too young, but I always had the impression there was something else. Was there?'

She caught her breath at the acuteness of his observation. She didn't know why she'd thought he would have noticed. He was giving her a chance to be honest, something she'd been wanting to do since he came back into her life.

She could do that now. Zoe had excused herself to go to bed, there were just the two of them.

'I didn't think . . . I didn't like Danny,' she admitted. Before Greg could say anything, she went on. 'I thought he was too . . . too self-absorbed. I was afraid he would leave when the show was over and break Zoe's heart. It would've been easy enough to do — she's emotionally vulnerable.'

'Like her mother at the same age, wouldn't you say?' he queried gently, looking at her over the rim of his cup.

Kay decided the conversation had become too personal and his eyes, too knowing. She set down her cup and stood up, hopeful that by putting a little distance between them she could control her erratic pulse-rate.

The first of the rain squalls rattled the house and beat against the windows. It gave her a reason to cross the room and crouch to ignite the gas fire.

'But, I was wrong about him, wasn't I?' she said, gazing reflectively into the blue flames for a moment before rising to face Greg. 'He didn't hurt Zoe, in fact, I think Zoe may have hurt him.'

Greg gave no sign he recognised her manoeuvre, not changing from his relaxed position on the couch.

'You're right about that. He obviously loved her.'

'It wasn't obvious to me until tonight. Men are so good at hiding their feelings. Why do they do that?' she asked.

'Would you rather we were all extroverted like Damien Riley?'

Damien Riley? How did he get into the conversation? Kay's brows drew together in a puzzled frown, but she decided against asking.

'Talking of change,' he went on, as if his question didn't need an answer. 'Have you thought over my suggestion that you sub-let the rooms above the tea-rooms?' he asked, leaning forward to take up the coffee pot. 'Do you want more coffee?'

She gave up fiddling with the ornaments on the mantle. 'Thank you,' she said, coming back to the couch. When she'd first settled beside him she answered his first question with one of her own.

'But will you be staying now?'

It was Greg's turn to look puzzled. 'Why wouldn't I? I told you of my plans.'

'But I thought they had to do with . . . I thought it was so as to be here for the wedding.'

'No, not just for that.'

There was a long silence, eventually broken by Greg.

'The sub-lease?' he prompted. 'Have you decided?'

Kay was glad to talk about business. It was safer 'Yes, I have thought about sub-letting,' she said. 'I've decided it would be a solution to the outrageous increase in rent I'm faced with. I don't want to give up the tea-rooms. Some of my people depend on me, and I like to be there for them.'

'So, you're to be my landlady,' he grinned. 'I like that.'

'There'll be strict rules, you understand. Break them and I can be the landlady from hell. No elephants, tigers or snakes allowed as pets, no washing your smalls in the bathroom — ' She broke off and stared at him, suddenly serious. 'You can't live there, the lease is strictly commercial . . . '

He answered her unspoken question matter-of-factly. 'No problem. I'll have to rent a flat.'

Kay searched his face. Encouraged by what she saw there, she took a chance, a big leap into the unknown.

'Do you have to look for somewhere else? As I see it, you'd be very handy in the kitchen. Unless brewing coffee and cooking roast lamb dinners are your only accomplishments.'

Greg pretended to be considering the offer. At least, she thought he was pretending. She no longer trusted her judgement where men were concerned, she had been wrong about Danny.

'Well, I expected to be moving out now I'm no longer needed as father-of-the-bride for the filming. But, yes, I would like to stay on. That way I'd be here for you when you become the mother-of-the-bride again.'

Hurriedly ridding herself of her empty coffee cup in a clatter of saucer and spoon, she threw up her hands with a tiny shriek of mock horror.

'Oh, no! Not more cameras, please!' she exclaimed, tumbling backwards on to the couch — and Greg.

He didn't move away.

'I have to remind you it could be for a very long time. We have three daughters,' he said, without missing a beat.

His voice lost its teasing as one arm reached out along the back of the couch to make her more comfortable against him. 'Would you mind that?'

Kay's body remembered her long, lean husband. She tucked her legs up under her and allowed herself to relax before answering him.

'Not as long as they don't bring home another film producer. I wouldn't like to go through that again.' She wrinkled her forehead. 'I wonder what will become of all that footage? It got Danny the job he wanted so I don't suppose it was wasted.'

Nothing was said for a long time. Outside, the wild weather continued its assault on the house, increasing the comfort of the warm room.

'This is nice,' Greg murmured, above her head.

'Mmmmmm.'

When the silence between them was broken a second time, they both spoke at once.

'You still wear your wedding — '

'What did you do to make Damien — '

They laughed at the confusion. 'After you,' he said.

Kay repeated her question. 'What did you do to make Damien call you Greta Garbo?'

Greg answered with a question of his own. 'Would he object to this?'

Kay jerked herself upright and half-turned to face him. 'Who, Damien? What is it with you and he?' she demanded.

'Nothing.'

'I don't believe you. You're always talking about him.'

She stared him into being candid.

'Would you believe I'm afraid?' he asked.

'Afraid? Of Damien? No, you'll have to do better than that.'

He shrugged. 'All right. It began on

the championship circuit. Journalists and managers get to see a lot of each other. He ... felt I was critical ... because I didn't share his love of late nights and booze and bragging ... and ... '

He gave a short laugh ... 'what he called babes. There were plenty of opportunities ... I didn't take them. He did his best to ... let's say I became a challenge to him. You know how it is.'

Kay waved a dismissive hand. She didn't want to hear any more about the journalist — she had heard enough. But she wanted to know more about Greg and his life in the years they were apart.

'Why didn't you take them? The opportunities?'

He frowned. 'Oh, come on, Kay, do I have to spell it out?'

There was only one reply to that.

'Yes,' she said, not willing to let him off the hook.

He looked uncomfortable. 'I could handle Damien's gibes on the tour, but when he began taking an interest in you and I wasn't sure how you felt about him, that was when I became afraid.'

Kay couldn't hide her disbelief. 'Of what?'

'I was afraid you might . . . fall for him. He's very successful with women.'

It didn't exactly answer her question of why he'd earned his nick-name, but she no longer cared. That was in the past and there were others to ask.

Unbelievable as the idea was, it seemed Greg had shown all the signs of being jealous. And she had been too blind to see it.

Was she brave enough to test her theory and risk learning she was wrong again?

'Why would it matter to you if I did?'

13

For a moment, Kay wondered if he was going to joke his way out of being truthful, either to save face or her feelings. Something in his eyes told her this was no joking matter to him. Steely resolve had replaced doubt.

'Because I never got over loving you,' he said, without hesitation. 'And I'm beginning to think, no, to hope you still love me.' He reached out and took her left hand and held it up for inspection. 'After all, you still wear my rings.'

Kay could only nod as she tried desperately to hold back the excitement that was threatening to overwhelm her. 'We are still married,' she managed to remind him.

'Yes,' he said simply.

A wave of delight surged through her as he lifted her hand to his lips, his questioning eyes on her face. What he read there seemed to please him. He kissed the narrow gold band and its matching diamond engagement ring.

The gesture brought Kay completely undone. She was being given another chance at happiness! Tears welled up, momentarily blurring her view of the loved face, the lump that rose in her throat almost choking the words that needed to be said.

'I'm so sorry . . . ' she gulped. 'I was wrong . . . to let you go . . . alone — '

'I was wrong to go, and I never stopped regretting it,' Greg broke in, almost harshly. 'I was a fool not to come back sooner, but I wanted to succeed, to show you. It got harder to admit the longer I left it.'

'And I was too proud . . . to call you back.'

With a gentle movement, he guided the hand he held to his shoulder and, almost tentatively, as if he still wasn't sure of her, gathered her into his embrace. Kay reached out her other hand to touch his face before sliding her arms around his neck.

The response was immediate — his hold on her tightened.

'We've wasted so many years,' he said fiercely in her ear.

Kay turned her head so that their lips met. The kiss unleashed a storm of emotion that rivalled the wild weather outside.

She realised the love she had tried so hard to forget throughout those lost years had deepened with maturity and the acceptance of her mistake.

'Could we start again?' she asked shakily after the urgency of the first kisses and protestations of love had eased.

'No, I think not,' Greg answered, but he was smiling into her startled eyes. 'We can't start again when we never stopped, can we?'

It made perfect sense to Kay. Reassured, she let go of her last doubts in a drawn-out sigh of contentment.

Greg took possession of her hands once more. 'You need an eternity ring to go with these,' he said, idly fingering her rings. 'I want to give you one.'

An eternity ring? Kay couldn't think of a more appropriate symbol of their love.

'I'd like that,' she said.

THE END

0	1	2	3	4	5	6	7	8	9
9510	801		993	364	365	346 507		518	0809
	901		9823	704		3057	268		
	0771		7953		960K	726	588		
			3073				808		
			943				1588		
						706	6557		
							9507 7978		
							9587		
							3087		

P10-L2061

thought of being able to drink a lovely cool glass of water at the turn of a tap was tantalizing.

As they were about to return to their rooms, Dorna's eyes were caught by a flash of dark blue blazer, as a man walked out of the lounge in the direction of the stairs. The man at the airport had worn a blue blazer. Her eyes followed the spot where he had disappeared. Was he staying at the same hotel? Hilary had said it was very popular with British people and they catered well to the British taste.

Then she gave herself a mental shake. What was she thinking about to be so affected by a complete stranger? And a man, too! She was off men. She had her work to think about, and that was enough for anyone.

At the door of her room she bade Hilary goodnight then, on impulse, before going to bed, she found her pad and pencil and did a number of sketches. Feeling better for having done something productive, she crawled into bed.

*　　　*　　　*

Over breakfast the following morning, Dorna showed Hilary her sketches and the older woman looked at them critically, but her enthusiasm seemed somewhat lacking. With heightened colour, Dorna was about to put them back in the folder when Hilary touched her hand.

'You might as well know,' she said. 'I shall have to rest up a day. A longish journey tires me nowadays, but all I need is a day to recover. Do you mind, my dear? I know there's a great deal you will wish to see, but...'

'There's plenty of time,' said Dorna, quickly. 'Of course you must rest up for a day. We'll get through everything that much more quickly tomorrow, I'm quite sure. And you've set us quite a programme as far as I can see. What would you like me to do? Shall I sit with you, or do you prefer to be on your own?'

'I like being on my own for an hour or two. I have some writing to do. But you ... well ... I don't like the thought of your wandering around on your own, Dorna. The natives would relieve you of your last penny if you don't know how to handle them.'

'Oh, Hilary, I think you exaggerate a lot. I shouldn't go far, but if you really like these drawings, I can improve upon them and perhaps do a few more. I think you ought to have plenty of preliminary ones to choose from. Where do we go tomorrow? Do you want the old or the new first?'

'We'd better do the old. Cairo first, maybe, then of course the pyramids, but I also want to look at present-day life in Egypt in the villages as well as the cities and contrast the ancient with the modern.'

'Right,' said Dorna, then she grinned. 'If

26

you do not see me back before dinner this evening, you'd better come looking for me.'

'Don't joke,' said Hilary, beginning to frown. 'Perhaps I should not have brought you after all. You are too young and attractive, and I'm a poor chaperone. I am bad at handling young girls.'

'Suppose a Moslem gentleman takes a fancy to me,' said Dorna, her eyes dancing, 'what shall I say? He is allowed four wives, isn't he?'

'Oh, off you go,' said Hilary. 'Just be careful, that's all.'

*   *   *

Dorna went out into the sunshine of Cairo. Across the road from the hotel was a camel station and she was immediately entreated to take a ride on a camel by one of the Arab drivers, but slowly she shook her head. That was a 'must' but for another day. She would prefer to have Hilary around before she sat one of these beasts. Instead she called a taxi and the driver beamed cheerfully and assured 'missie' that he could take her to the centre of Cairo in no time.

'To the Museum,' he agreed. 'All missies want to see the Museum.'

Dorna did not dissuade him, though she knew she would also leave that until she and Hilary could go together. This morning she wanted bazaars and street scenes which she

27

could savour by herself. She had an idea that Hilary had done her browsing a long time ago, and had no time for such frivolous pursuits nowadays. She was a very dedicated professional lady.

The traffic made Dorna stare. At times there was no movement at all and the driver apparently had all the time in the world. He gave Dorna 'plenty information' and was quite frank that having pleased missie he expected a good tip. Dorna looked out at the honking cars, the horses, oxen, carts of every description shape and size, many of which she decided must be home-made. On one cart a farmer, with what appeared to be his entire family, sat on the cart loaded with vegetables on the way to market. Dorna's pencil was kept busy as they all began to move slowly in the same direction.

'What do you call the scarf and head-ring which the men wear?' she asked the driver.

'Caffea and egal,' he nodded. 'Women wear black clothes.'

'I can see that,' said Dorna, drily.

Everywhere new buildings were being thrown up with the traditional mud bricks still being used. They were indeed the greatest of all contrasts to the wonderful pyramids of Ancient Egypt, these buildings which looked like dolls' houses being piled on top of one another. How long would they last? Dorna wondered. How many would look beautiful on completion?

'The American Embassy, missie,' the driver informed her. 'You not American? No dollars?'

'No,' said Dorna, firmly, finding the money which Hilary had recommended, enough to please her driver and no more. 'This will do.'

There were bazaars straight across from the American Embassy, and Dorna's cheeks warmed with excitement as she plunged into the crowds. All thoughts of Mark had completely gone from her head as she began to explore and to sketch the wonderful, colourful scenes. Flies were everywhere and mournful dogs were specially prone to the pests, but Dorna brushed them aside as she drew small, near-naked children with huge eyes of great beauty, and by contrast old, wrinkled faces full of character and a lifetime of living. Perhaps because she was so interested, she could feel happiness around her in spite of the dirt, and her eyes shone like lamps.

She had eaten little for breakfast, but now Dorna's stomach tightened with hunger, though Hilary had warned her to be careful about food. She should eat nothing which was unwrapped or could not be peeled.

One stall was selling melons and Dorna had no hesitation in buying one. Inside her bag she carried a small pocket knife and a packet of tissues. The melon would quench her thirst as well as satisfying her hunger. Clutching it in her arms, she looked around for a suitable place to sit, when suddenly her arm was gripped and her heart bounded with fright.

'You mustn't eat it,' a deep voice said in her ear.

Dorna whirled round and saw that the man she had noticed at the airport was now standing beside her and that his steady amber eyes once again looked into her own.

'I ... I beg your pardon,' she said, breathlessly. 'I've only just bought it. It is not over-ripe...'

'No, but an injection has been used in ripening the fruit. I will examine the melons and show you which one you can buy. It will be equally delicious, I promise you, but that one might upset you. Give it to one of these urchins.'

But that, too, was a mistake in that it brought an army of small youngsters crowding after her, and clamouring for money.

'You seem to have lifted me out of the frying pan into the fire,' she said, ruefully.

'Not quite,' he admitted. 'I think I'm only a little ahead of you in knowing my Egypt! My name, by the way, is Simon Elliott.'

'Jane Dorning,' she said.

'How do you do, Miss Dorning.'

'Generally I'm called "Dorna".'

'Then, hello Dorna, nice name. Where is your companion today?'

Suddenly she felt he was asking rather a lot

of questions. He looked nice and reliable, but how could she be sure? Hadn't Hilary told her to be wary of becoming involved with *anyone*?

'Miss Grant is resting,' she said, rather stiffly. 'She's a colleague. Now, if you will excuse me, Mr Elliott.'

He grinned and she had the horrible feeling that he could read her mind. His hand was on her arm again, guiding her through the bazaar stalls.

'I don't think so, Miss Dorna. At least, not until I see you safely back to your hotel. Egypt is a beautiful, highly cultured and civilized country, but you do have to understand it. Your colleague, Miss Grant, needs her head examining for letting a young girl like you out on your own in Cairo. She should know better. You'd have eaten that particular melon and spent some of your precious holiday time feeling sick with gyppy tummy, and God knows what else if you think you can eat what you like.'

'I'm not on holiday!' she said, angrily.

'Well, all the more reason to keep healthy.' He was still smiling and there was warmth in his eyes, but now Dorna could see that he was looking at her with a hint of impatience. No doubt she was just a nuisance and he felt responsible for her because she was English.

'Really, Mr Elliott, I can take a taxi.'

'And find yourself having to argue over the tip? You might have been lucky getting here,

31

but not so lucky getting back. Are you hungry? Was that why you were buying the melon? You'd better come with me and I'll buy you some food ... No, I can see that won't do!' he added, as a dangerous light shone in her eyes, '... I will supervise what *you* buy for yourself, and perhaps you will allow me to share your table if I buy my own bread.'

'I don't want a big lunch,' she protested. 'A salad will do.'

'I'll supervise the salad, unless we eat it at the hotel.'

'Cheese, then.'

'The good square white cheese. Butter only if wrapped, though the bread is lovely. I will allow you to eat the bread, and you can have bananas, if you like.'

'Thank you very much,' she said in a small voice, and this time he smiled at her again. It was certainly a new approach, she thought, for getting to know a girl and much more effective than a dropped handkerchief!

'Don't sulk,' he was saying. 'I know that ... I mean I have no doubt that Miss Grant is a seasoned traveller and will feel better tomorrow and you won't need to put up with my company, but today you accept my unwanted attentions. Okay? You have eyes like pools of beautiful clear water, Miss Dorna. Very cooling for such a hot day.'

She refused to look into his own teasing orbs.

'Where is your own lady companion?' she asked, pointedly, and he grinned.

'So you *did* notice me at the airport, just as I noticed you. It's called attraction, you know. It can be quite dynamic, and it can happen very suddenly. I think, perhaps, it has happened to me. Now let's see what you can have for lunch.'

Dorna looked at his dancing eyes and decided he was teasing her. She only wanted rolls with the cheese he recommended and a bottle of clear cool water. She decided to allow Hilary to choose her food from now on if it was really true that Egyptian food could be upsetting.

But Simon Elliott seemed to dominate over her as he sat opposite to her in a delightful restaurant as Victorian as the hotel.

'Tell me about yourself,' he invited.

'Nothing to tell.'

'There must be *something*. Where do you live? Have you a family?'

'My father is dead and Mother has married again. I have no brothers or sisters. I look after myself.'

'All by yourself?'

The tone was probing and she flushed.

'I don't like that sort of question.'

This time it was his turn to look discomfited.

'I apologise ... truly. It's just that I feel I want to know all about you, Dorna, and that there is so little time when one meets a girl under these circumstances. I could allow you to walk out of here and . . .' he spread his hands, '. . . and never see you again. I don't want that to happen.'

He stared into her eyes, and strange things began to happen to Dorna's heart. It was completely mad, but although she had sworn never even to look at another man, this man was almost forcing her to look at him, and to be interested in him. Her heart was beating very fast, and the colour came and went in her cheeks.

'We are complete strangers, Mr Elliott. Why should I tell you anything? I know nothing at all about you.'

'Simon. Call me Simon. I'm quite respectable. I do research for television programmes and that is a respectable enough occupation. I certainly want to get to know you rather better.'

'I think you must be making fun of me,' she said, breathlessly. He must be about the most handsome man she had ever seen, she thought, as her artist's eye took in the shape of his head, his strong features and the vitality of his personality.

'Why do you say that? You must know that you are very beautiful, and I am very direct. I get used to discarding what is irrelevant in my work. I also do the same thing with you. Why beat about the bush? I want us to be friends, so I am making my position clear to you.'

Dorna felt as though she were being rushed

towards some sort of whirlpool, and she had to fight desperately against it.

'I would like to go back to my hotel,' she told him.

'*Our* hotel. I am also booked into that same hotel. Very well, if you want to be all formal and stand-offish, I must accept it. Though ...' his eyes twinkled, '... what a waste. Didn't you see those pyramids last night, by moonlight? Didn't they stir you just a little? Didn't you think they looked romantic?'

She made no answer. Once again she found herself in a taxi on the way back to the hotel at Giza. Her emotions were so disturbed that she hardly listened to the conversation between their driver and Simon Elliott. She did not know how to treat him. He was no doubt here on business, but she would hardly have thought he was starved of feminine company! Perhaps that girl at the airport had given him the brush-off!

Well, she was not here to provide Mr Elliott with his entertainment either. If his senses had been roused, as had her own, by the sight of so much beauty in the moonlight, then he would have to find some other girl.

'Thank you for bringing me home,' she said to him, formally, when they reached the hotel 'I must go and attend to Miss Grant. Goodbye, Mr Elliott.'

'Simon. 'Voir, Dorna. Maybe it's going to take a determined man to get to know you, but

I am very determined.'

'So am I,' she said, quietly, as she turned away.

CHAPTER FOUR

For a reason she could not quite explain to herself, Dorna hardly mentioned Simon Elliott to Hilary beyond telling her that a young Englishman staying at the hotel had assisted her in getting a taxi back from Cairo. Hilary had asked if she 'sneaked men up to her room' and she had denied it firmly, but this was something very different yet she felt shy of telling her about Simon Elliott.

'There's heaps of material there, Hilary,' she said, after ensuring that the older woman had now recovered her stamina after a good rest. She had produced the folder she had taken with her to the bazaars.

Hilary found her rather thick spectacles and began to leaf over the sketches, though again with less enthusiasm than Dorna had expected. But she was getting more used to Hilary Grant, and she knew that silence did not necessarily mean disapproval. Sometimes it meant that Hilary was deep in thought.

'I saw you arriving back here with that young man,' she said, suddenly. 'I think I've seen him before somewhere.'

'You did. It was at the...'

'Did you pick him up, Dorna? I know you're young and attractive but you've hardly been here five minutes before you're coming home with strange young men in tow. Running after men won't keep your mind on the job.'

Dorna's face had gone white.

'I am *not* running after any man,' she said, clearly. 'The gentleman is staying at this hotel. He felt I ought not to walk around on my own.'

'So it's *my* fault now!'

'No, of course not. I didn't say that. But you're making too much of it. I am *not* interested in Mr Elliott and I *am* interested in my work. But I don't think...'

She hesitated, wondering how to put over her point of view. Surely she was a free agent? Hilary Grant could not dictate to her over her friends. She should be free to be friends with whom she liked.

But already the older woman was smiling ruefully as she reached out and put a hand over Dorna's.

'I told you I was a bad-tempered old woman,' she said. 'I'm sorry. It's just that I had hoped to plan out some work today but it has not gone right for me. As I say, I lash out at anything in sight when I feel frustrated, and it happened to be yourself.'

Dorna nodded. 'You did warn me.'

'And I happen to believe that love affairs can be a great handicap on a project of this sort.

37

They interfere badly with creative work.'

'Not mine!' Dorna denied.

She felt irritated with herself, with Miss Grant, and with Simon Elliott, all three. There was no need for Hilary to go jumping to conclusions, and although she had warned Dorna that she was difficult to live with at times, the reality might not be too comfortable. Dorna was used to a quiet life.

And as for Simon Elliott, she would have to avoid him at all costs, because in spite of her protests to Hilary, she could not stop herself from thinking about him.

She glanced round the people in the hotel lounge that evening, but there was no sign of his tall figure or the sound of his deep voice, and she was furious with herself because she could not control her own deep disappointment. What did she know about him? she asked herself, crossly. Absolutely nothing. He could easily be a charming crook.

Dorna was not at peace with herself when she went to bed that night. This project was not going to be as easy as she had imagined.

There was no signs of bad temper when Hilary Grant arrived down to breakfast the following morning. She was full of brisk energy and enthusiasm.

'I have hired a car for us, Dorna,' she said brightly. 'There is a village not too far away where I understand excavation is going on at the moment. They have found statues of

Rameses II. That is quite a good point to make a start. I can do a chapter on Rameses who built quite a number of statues to himself, and you can do a few sketches of the excavations, then we can contrast it with the village life all around. What do you say?'

'I'm happy with that,' Dorna agreed, though her tone was rather cool. Hilary had apparently forgotten that they had ever had a cross word, and after a hot drink and some croissants, Dorna put her own ruffled feelings behind her and began to plan her day.

The statue of Rameses was in excellent condition and appeared to have been carved out of marble.

'We will be doing rather a lot on Rameses II,' said Hilary, 'and looking at his most famous statues later, so I think a separate folder for him, Dorna. Can you emphasize this point, and this?'

Dorna quickly sketched in every detail of interest to Hilary but her own interest lay in the village life going on all around; the huts made of mud bricks with flat roofs, the women wearing black robes with their faces covered and some carrying jugs of water on their heads. Her pencil flew over her pad as she tried to capture the fascination of the place. She sketched men in long robes, people riding small donkeys with their legs almost dangling to the ground, dogs everywhere, farmers ploughing their fields with wooden ploughs and oxen, and children running about half-naked.

She was busy sketching women washing their clothes in the Nile when Hilary came to find her.

'I wish to photograph one of the water-wheels which is drawing up water to irrigate the fields. Can you do a few sketches as well, please?'

She indicated a large wheel with earthenware crocks tied to it at various points. An ox was pulling another wheel which lay flat, about two feet off the ground and which operated the first, and a little girl sat happily behind the ox, keeping it going with a whip.

'Try to capture the child's face,' Hilary said. 'I doubt if she inflicts much damage on the ox, but she is a happy child.'

And a happy village, thought Dorna, as she saw many smiling faces.

'They have a problem with irrigation,' Hilary was saying.

Dorna nodded. She remembered that Mark had spent some time in Egypt just before she met him. It was strange that she could think of him now without pain. He seemed so far away. That old life might have happened in another existence. Had his irrigation project helped other people? Had Mark now gone to Scotland? Was he married now?

And what about Simon Elliott? He was so very good-looking. Dorna paused for a long time, lost in thought, then she came to her senses with a start. She must not day-dream about Simon Elliott. He meant nothing to her. Perhaps even now his conference, or whatever had brought him to Egypt, would be over and he would have checked out of the hotel and be on his way back to London. Perhaps she would never see him again.

Even as the thought came, her heart lurched. She was finding it difficult to control her own emotions, because she knew that she wanted to see Simon Elliott again very much.

When Hilary decided that they had done enough for one day, Dorna breathed a sigh of relief and readily agreed to return to their hotel.

'What do you think would happen if those on research, or those working on irrigation like Mark, succeeded in growing things in the desert?' she asked Hilary.

'More of everything,' said Hilary. 'More camels, more children, more mouths to feed, more starvation.'

'Oh Hilary, you are a Jeremiah,' Dorna laughed.

'Well, you asked,' said Hilary, rather tartly. She was becoming tired again, but she looked sideways at Dorna. What was that young man doing in Egypt? Was he working on irrigation? He reminded her of someone . . . something . . . and it was not a happy memory. Where *had* she seen him before. Hilary shook her head, knowing that her memory was becoming very

41

poor these days. She hoped that Dorna was not going to fall in love and moon around when she should be working. It was almost as bad as drink, thought Hilary sourly.

Then she smiled at herself. Just because she once had a fiancé who had turned out to be a rotter, and who had made her love him when he already had a wife and children, did not mean that all men were so unprincipled. She must get to know this man. In fact, there could be something in it for her. Learning about other people was always a prime source of good material.

CHAPTER FIVE

After the first night of their arrival, Hilary had decreed that she and Dorna would respect one another's privacy and that once they were each in their own rooms, there would be no contact with one another, except in dire emergency.

This had seemed strange to Dorna at first, but now she welcomed it. She found it relaxing to be entirely on her own for an hour or two each evening. In the mornings they met over breakfast in the diningroom, and on the following morning when she went downstairs, she found that another guest was sharing their table, and that Hilary was in earnest conversation with Simon Elliott.

He rose to his feet when she came to join them, his amber eyes fixed on her face. Dorna suddenly wished she had paid more attention to her make-up, though she hoped she looked clean and fresh.

'You did not tell me Mr Elliott was a television man,' Hilary said, almost accusingly.

Dorna's mouth fell open and she was about to confess that she knew very little about Simon Elliott when her eyes met his and she decided to say nothing. Hilary was always full of surprises, she decided.

'Nothing to get excited about,' he said, easily. 'I'm only here for preliminary purposes. Cairo possesses the oldest university in the world and in 1988 it will be a thousand years old. At the moment I am on research for a television programme on the Middle East and I decided to find out whilst I am in the vicinity if there is something in it for us; some sort of programme to mark the event. One or two people are also interested and we are arranging a few meetings to have discussions and so on. Nothing cut-and-dried as yet.'

'Nevertheless it is very exciting,' said Hilary. 'I'm most interested in television myself. That's so, isn't it, Dorna?'

She was certainly much more affable over Simon Elliott this morning than she had been last night! Dorna remembered Liz Paige remarking that Hilary would love to see one of her books being made into a television programme for children.

'That is so,' she agreed.

'I understand you are here on a project of your own,' Simon Elliott said, though his eyes quickly moved to Dorna and she blushed at the intensity of his gaze. His eyes were almost golden in the morning light and his hair curled closely to his head. She longed to pull out each curl and watch it spring back into place. His shoulders were broad, and she could imagine that he would have great strength in his arms. His mouth, too, was well-shaped and she wondered what it would be like to be held in his arms, and to feel his kisses...

'Dorna? Dorna!' Hilary was saying, impatiently, and Dorna blushed to the roots of her hair. What was happening to her when she had such thoughts about Simon Elliott, especially after all that had happened between herself and Mark? How humiliated she would feel if he could read her mind. Already he no doubt thought her a fool for wandering around Cairo on her own.

'I ... I'm sorry,' she said. 'I'm not quite awake yet. I'm afraid I am more of an owl than a lark.'

'You said you wanted to ride on a camel and I've no intention of allowing myself to be coaxed into sitting on one of those beasts. I have some notes to write up. Why don't you go with Mr Elliott who is also determined to ride on a camel? We can then have lunch together

44

and we'll go and look at one or two of the pyramids this afternoon.'

Dorna was shaking her head. She had no intention of inflicting herself on Simon Elliott at any time, and certainly not through Hilary's machinations. In any case she had made up her mind to pay her own expenses while she was in Egypt. She could afford it ... just. She would have her fees from the book, and she did not want to be beholden to Hilary Grant. She was not Hilary's employee. They were colleagues and she must not allow the older woman to run her life, but she had seen rather quickly that Hilary might try to do just that if she were not very firm with her, and remained independent.

'I don't think so, thank you,' she said, pleasantly. 'I am here to do a job and I would prefer to get on with it, Hilary. I will be happy to ride on a camel, but not until after all the work is done. I don't want to spend too much time in Egypt. I shall have other work waiting for me when I get back.'

'You agreed to come for as long as it takes,' Hilary reminded her. 'I shall hold you to that, Dorna.'

'All work and no play,' intoned Simon Elliott. 'I can't imagine you would ever be a dull girl, Dorna, but don't let's give it a chance. Come on, let's get on our nice camels and you can enjoy quite a new experience. We will likely have to join a queue of tourists, but it could be fun. I'm sure you can catch up on your work quite easily, as I shall have to do.'

His eyes were gleaming with laughter. Somewhere a warning voice was advising Dorna not to go, not to allow him any bigger hold on her interest. She'd had enough of men with the way Mark had behaved to her, and she was astonished and rather ashamed that she could allow this man to capture her interest so soon after Mark had bruised her heart. She had loved Mark, hadn't she? Her greatest desire had been to marry him so that they could spend the rest of their lives together. She had been devastated when he did not feel the same way.

But now she could feel her senses stirring every time Simon Elliott looked at her, and when he leaned over to touch her arm, she pulled away as though his fingers had been alive with electricity.

'Very well, no camel ride,' he laughed. 'It's probably too childish anyway for Miss Dorna? It's too much the tourist attraction.'

Dorna felt that she was being stuffy. Hilary was looking at her rather balefully, as she did when she was being thwarted.

'I still have to write up my notes,' she reiterated.

'Oh, okay then, I'll go,' said Dorna.

'Good girl,' said Simon Elliott, softly. 'I knew you were game for a little fun.'

'That depends on the fun,' she told him. 'As I say, I'm here to work. I can get all the fun I want in London.'

46

'So can I, but we are not there now. By the way, *I'll* do the tip. Those Arab drivers would have you buying the camel.'

They crossed the road to the camel station and once again Dorna forgot everything in her enchantment at the busy scene in front of her. It seemed like a huge motley moving crowd of camels, Arabs, flies, dust and noise.

'Can you wait for a moment?' she asked, breathlessly, and whipped her pad out of her bag. With swift skilful strokes she captured the essential ingredients of the scene. Perhaps Hilary would use it later when she had done her final copy, and perhaps not, but she would enjoy keeping it for her own records. Her urge to get things down on paper was always irresistible and she worked quickly and with absorption.

'You were not pretending,' said Simon at her elbow. 'You really *do* want to work. These are good. It's your way of earning your living, of course.'

'I'm not trying to prove anything,' she said, as she slashed in the last of her strokes. 'I only know when I *have* to get things down. Since you want me to accompany you, you'll have to be prepared to wait for me now and again.'

'A career woman, then. Are you dedicated to your work, Dorna?'

'Do you mean *entirely* dedicated?'

'That's exactly what I mean.'

'You ask a great many questions. You

47

always seem to be asking me questions.'

'I shall ask one more. How about dinner?'

She stared incomprehendingly. 'Dinner?'

'Sure. Do you also bring along your pad and pencil so that no sooner do we start the soup than you are sketching the fellow eating corn with butter at the next table.'

She laughed. 'No, there are limits. I do put aside my work in the evenings, unless I want to work from my sketches. If I have an editor waiting for work, I often do overtime to turn it out.'

'You freelance?'

She nodded. 'I like variety.'

'In everything? Does that also apply to the men in your life, or is there someone to whom you have pledged undying love?'

She coloured. 'That would be none of your business.'

'Perhaps I want to make it my business,' he said, softly.

He took her arm and she turned quickly to where the Arab drivers were exhorting them to take the next camel.

'I don't think we're allowed to pick and choose,' she said, and he laughed.

'What a pity! I always like to pick and choose.'

'I dare say you have plenty of women ready to allow you to pick and choose,' she said, sweetly.

'I am talking about camels,' he returned.

Dorna's camel turned to look at her carefully. Blinking his long lashes, he turned away again disdainfully and she laughed.

'Apparently I'm not worth looking at,' she said, but it was the Arab driver who was standing beside her and not Simon.

'Oh, missie, I show,' he said. 'Put purse over front. Lean forward.'

She put her leg over the camel's hump and almost immediately he started to get up; first his front legs so that she had to lean forward, then the back legs and she leaned backwards, finally straightening herself in the saddle.

She looked behind and saw that Simon Elliott was also mounted, and thought it a pity he was not wearing flowing white robes. He would have looked splendid, she thought.

The camel ambled off, swaying like a boat in motion. His two left legs moved together, then the two right. Dorna began to relax and to enjoy herself, and when the driver called out that he would take a picture, the camel stopped obligingly. She laughed and the driver was delighted.

'I please missie,' he said, holding out his hand. She looked at him, well aware that she was being asked for a tip. How much did one give? If she gave too much, would she have the same experience as yesterday with many hands being held out asking for more.

'That's enough,' Simon called out. 'I'll attend to the tip. Missie with me. No tip until the pyramids.'

The driver gave Dorna a look of disgust, but she clung to the camel until they reached the pyramids where the beast went down so suddenly that she was startled, and almost fell off. But already Simon was beside her, paying the driver with Egyptian money.

'They like either Egyptian money or American green stuff,' he said. 'No silver. If you had offered him silver, he might have turned nasty. How did you like your camel ride?'

'We go back to the hotel by taxi,' she said, laughing. 'It was an experience, but I prefer modern transport. I did admire my camel's long eyelashes, though.'

'Your own aren't half-bad,' said Simon, and again took her arm. 'Are you going to climb the biggest of the pyramids? You'd better think twice if you can't stand heights or close quarters, or if you puff and blow going upstairs.'

'I'm an old wreck,' she grinned. 'Can't you see that? I'll probably have hysterics half-way up.'

'Not with me to look after you. That's why it is better for you to come with me and not with Miss Grant. She's quite a lady, though.'

There was a meaningful note in his voice and Dorna looked at him quickly.

'You've known her before?'

'Hardly that. I ... ah ... I was acquainted

with her in a professional capacity.'

'She's very successful as a writer,' she told him. 'Her books do well. I don't think she is given the recognition she is due.'

'Her books require to be well illustrated,' said Simon. 'The illustrations count for a great deal. People buy them for those as much as for the text.'

'Then you know her *books* well?'

'Oh yes, quite well,' he said, briefly. 'Now, Dorna, here we are. Take my hand and we'll join this party.'

They climbed a few steps outside the pyramid, then entered a dimly lit tunnel. On either side, along the walls, sat guides clad in their native dress, one of them rising to join the head of their party.

They climbed a ramp then bent over, entering a tunnel which was very narrow, with boards set crossways for a foothold.

'Remain bent,' Simon called, 'or you may crack your head.'

Dorna could see why he had warned her that she might find it claustrophobic, but soon they were out of the tunnel and with a sigh of relief, she stood upright again.

They climbed a few rungs of a ladder, then on to the next ramp where they could walk standing up. Holding on to a railing at one side, they could look down into a pit below.

'I can't see anything,' said Dorna. 'It's too dim.'

'You will in a moment.'

They walked up another ramp and in a moment they were in the tomb of Cheops, and for a moment Dorna stood breathless, suddenly very much aware of the thousands and thousands of men who had laboured to build the great pyramids and the years it had taken to build them.

The Pyramid of Cheops was huge, the walls made of pink Aswan granite. It was an experience, thought Dorna, as she leaned up against a table behind the sarcophagus, but one of the senses rather than the eye. Her senses were sharpened to a degree by the grandeur and the wonder of the place.

Simon had put an arm round her shoulders to support her during the climb, and now he pulled her against him.

'No two people who have shared a climb to the Pyramid of Cheops can be indifferent to one another,' he whispered. 'We must get to know one another very well, you and I. Don't you agree, Dorna?'

'I . . .' She hardly knew what to reply. Her heart was beating wildly at his closeness.

'How do we get down?'

'Same way, of course.'

'Then we'd best follow the party.'

Suddenly he bent his head and for a brief moment his lips touched her lightly. Dorna's heart raced loudly enough for them both to hear!

'We *must* go,' she said, nervously. 'We must follow the others.'

She could feel the strength of his hands on her shoulders, then a moment later he was kissing her bruisingly and her knees seemed to turn to water. Her whole body seemed to surge madly with excitement as she was imprisoned in his arms and one of his hands held her firmly at the back of her neck. Then with a movement which was almost violent, she pushed him away.

'For God's sake, we ... we must follow the others!'

'You're frightened,' he said, softly. 'You're frightened of me, Dorna.'

He laughed softly, and again her heart hammered with fear as she sought to make the descent, step by step, until she once again came out into the fresh air. She was not sure that she had any reason to be frightened of Simon Elliott, but she was afraid of the way he could touch her emotions so easily. But there was a great deal about him that she did not know. In fact, she knew *nothing* about him, beyond what he had told her and Hilary. Yet she had the strange feeling that picking her up was no accident. He had known who she was, just as he knew Hilary. Yet why should he be interested in her? She had nothing to offer anyone, except her work, and Simon Elliott was unlikely to be interested in that, except superficially.

Behind her Simon kept a hand on her shoulders as they passed their guide who had turned to meet the party with hand outstretched for his tip.

'Oh no, this time I pay my own,' said Dorna, making the tip a sizeable one.

'Too much,' grinned Simon. 'It doesn't do to give people too much.'

'I believe you,' she said, drily, and he caught her arm.

'Don't tell me you were not stirred in your heart,' he said, softly, 'because I know better.'

'Apparently you are very experienced where women are concerned,' she said, coldly. 'Well, I don't intend to be added to your list of conquests. Or can it be that you are married and like to play the field a little when you shake free of domesticity?'

'No wife,' he assured her. 'Not any more.'

'Then you are divorced?'

They were moving towards the area where buses awaited the tourists and where Simon hoped to hire a car to return to the hotel. Suddenly a small sandstorm blew up and Dorna gasped as she felt something like small needles hitting her face.

Simon pulled her into his arms, shielding her.

'Over here,' he said, guiding her towards a building which housed a boat which had been taken from one of the tombs. 'I had arranged for us to come here in any case. It is only a little sandstorm.'

Dorna breathed more easily and put up a hand to her face.

'I'm okay. It was just unexpected, that's all.'

'Sometimes the most unexpected things can be the most exciting,' he told her. 'Take this boat, for instance. It is 4,500 years old and was only dug up in 1954. Don't you think it is rather incongruous to find a boat here? I've had to get special permission, by the way, for us to see this so you can sketch it all carefully. It transported the mummy of Cheops down the Nile before being dismantled, and when it was found it had the shipwright's instructions on it as to how it should be reassembled. Doesn't it make you feel that our own little lives are very short-lived, Dorna? Doesn't it make you feel that it is a crime to waste a moment of the time allotted to us?'

But already her fingers were itching and she drew her pad and pencil out of her bag and began to sketch furiously.

'Don't talk to me for a moment,' she said, quickly. 'I have work to do. I must get this down.'

'Do you never take photographs, Dorna?' he asked after a few minutes when she had sketched most of what she wanted.

'Sometimes. Rarely, though. I find I can get all I need from my sketch pad, then I work on it later. I have an almost photographic memory of things and can conjure it all up in my mind whenever I want. I've tried to train myself to do this over the years.'

'Shut your eyes,' he commanded and she did so.

'What colour are my eyes?' he asked.

'Light brown, almost golden. Some people would say they were amber.'

'Very good. Unobservant people notice eyes, but can rarely tell the colour if leapt upon to do so quickly. Yours are clear grey, like a mountain stream. I notice them all the time.'

He was laughing at her again. She could tell from the light tones in his voice.

'My wife was a photographer,' he volunteered.

'Professionally?'

He nodded. 'She was very good.'

'Has she given it up, then?'

'You could say that,' he nodded, but this time there was a closed look to his face and she knew she could not question him further. He could be a formidable man, she decided, when he wished.

A hired car was waiting for them and they returned to the hotel, almost in silence. Where was his wife now? she wondered. Had she married someone else? Did he still love her?

She told herself, firmly, that she did not want to know and that Simon Elliott must remain a complete stranger to her, a man she did not want to know. He upset her too much.

'Ships that pass in the night,' she murmured

to herself. That was how she must think of him.

Back at the hotel he saw her to the elevator, which was working that day but only to the second floor.

'I have to go now,' he told her. 'I have some business meetings, but I hope to see you this evening.'

'I shall be having dinner with Hilary Grant.'

'I know,' he said, heavily. 'You are both working together this afternoon. I . . .'

He paused and looked at her very thoughtfully.

'Mind how you go, Dorna. I shall see you . . . both of you . . . later.'

CHAPTER SIX

Hilary had delayed eating her lunch until Dorna arrived back at the hotel and now they shared a table where they both tucked into a nicely-cooked meal of chicken with various vegetables, all of which had been cooked in boiling water.

'If I continue to live on rolls and bottled water, I shall be like a skeleton by the time we get back,' said Dorna. 'It's nice to eat something well cooked again. Simon says we must be careful about salads and only certain cheese and butter only if wrapped. No melons either unless he examines them, yet they all look so delicious.'

'They also pick up bacteria from irrigation,' said Hilary. 'Well?'

'Well what?'

'Did you have a nice morning? Tell me about the camel ride and what did you think of the Pyramid of Cheops? I've been there several times myself, so there's no need for me to go back. I've all the information I need on that. But I would like to hear about Simon Elliott. I have such a strange feeling at the back of my mind about him. Did he tell you all about himself? I asked him if we had met before but we were interrupted by the waiter, then you came. Did he tell you anything at all?'

'Not really. I found the camel ride quite an experience and the tomb was a bit claustrophobic, though very impressive.'

'But what about Simon?'

'There's nothing much to tell,' said Dorna, with slightly heightened colour. What could she say? That he had kissed her so that her senses had jangled like alarm bells? That he had golden eyes which reminded her of a jungle animal, yet she wanted him around and felt that she had lost something when he walked away from her. It reminded her of her childhood when her parents sometimes went out for the evening, and she was left feeling lost and lonely, even in the care of a nursemaid, until they returned home. At the same time, she did not want him around because he had the power to confuse her so much that she did not know what she was doing. She did not know what she wanted with regard to Simon Elliott. There was something reassuring about his tall, very handsome figure, but she kept reminding herself that she must not again lose her heart to a man. She'd had enough with Mark!

'There must be *something* to tell,' Hilary was saying, impatiently.

The more they worked together, the more a querulous note was beginning to creep into Hilary Grant's voice. Dorna thought she understood this. The older woman was creative. She had already warned Dorna that she could become bad-tempered when she was on the job, and although Dorna had thought she might be exaggerating, now she was not quite so sure.

'We only joined a party being shown through the largest pyramid, then later I sketched the boat which was dug up in 1954, the boat used to bring the mummified remains of Cheops down the Nile. We came back to the hotel and Simon . . . Mr Elliott . . . went off on business of his own. And here I am, ready for us both to do some work together this afternoon.'

'Hm.'

Hilary Grant looked reflective.

'You got along okay with him, then?'

'Certainly I did, though I'm sure Mr Elliott must have friends of his own here.'

'I feel...' said Hilary, slowly, and she seemed to be deep in thought. 'I feel that I should know Simon Elliott from somewhere. I feel that I have met him before, though he says we have not met. I also feel that he is a much more important man in his own field than he pretends. He could do a lot for us, Dorna. If we could get a programme on television from one of my books ... your drawings, too, of course ... then we would be sure of success.'

'You are successful already,' Dorna told her, 'and I'm only concerned to keep myself in steady work. I've always believed that supporting actors and actresses remain in work longer than the stars. They don't all remain at the top for ever. I'll settle for a steady flow of bread and butter instead of being stuffed with cake for a short while, then allowed to starve.'

'Well, I've been on bread and butter for years ... with regard to my work, that is. Fortunately I had my own money from my parents. But I only appeal to a certain section of the reading public, mainly children, even though I've tried various experiments and have become exceedingly frustrated if they do not turn out as I would wish. I've worked with very stupid people, Dorna. A man said I drove him to drink. Nonsense. He was already very familiar with the stuff. And a stupid girl hired to take photographs was impertinent. She said I only used prose to link up her photographs. I saw to it that I did not have to work with *her* again. I do have some influence, you know.'

'But not for television,' said Dorna, her eyes crinkling.

For a moment Hilary stared at her rather malevolently.

'Not for television,' she agreed, 'yet women older than I am have made their debut on television. Look at Barbara Woodhouse. She's my age, or older, and she's a star. She even puts out books which sell. All I need is a bit of luck, and meeting the right person, and something tells me it might be Simon Elliott. I'm hoping you will become friendly with him, Dorna.'

'You warned me against him at first.'

Hilary looked pained. 'Yes, but that was *before* I knew he was a television man. He is the first television man that I have met.'

Dorna drew a deep breath. Was she hearing properly? Hilary Grant was actually suggesting that she should cultivate Simon Elliott in order to influence him into getting Hilary a spot on television!

She wanted to laugh heartily, but some instinct told her to remain calm and take things easy. Hilary would not appreciate her laughter.

'I don't think Simon Elliott would become *that* much interested in me,' she said, after a pause.

'I think he would,' said Hilary, eagerly. 'I saw the way he looked at you, and if I'm any judge of men, he is the sort who likes women. I bet they fawn all over him because of his job . . .

and his looks as well, of course. If I could take off forty-odd years, I would be trying to give you a run for your money.'

Dorna looked down at her plate. Hilary was being waggish and she found this embarrassing.

'You could influence him if you tried, Dorna.'

'Well I don't want to try,' said Dorna. 'I should hate to be so underhand, and I'm sure he would guess.'

'Underhand!'

Again there was a look in Hilary's black eyes which she found disturbing. She was beginning to think that she had another description for her older colleague as well as bad-tempered. Hilary was spoilt with all her money. She was used to buying everything she wanted, and perhaps, even, she had spent a little of it in buying success. What exactly did the 'influence' she kept talking about encompass?

But again the older woman was smiling.

'I'm only thinking of your having a happy time while you are in Egypt, my dear,' she said, mildly. 'Your drawings are excellent, and I'm sure you will work even better if you find an attractive friend who can take you about after we have set out to accomplish our work together. I like time to myself in the evenings, but it must be dull for a young girl like you, and I don't want you getting mixed up with some worthless young man. One reason why I think

Simon Elliott would be good for you is certainly *because* of his job. It means he is a man of stature, with a profession. You don't want to waste your time on some young construction worker who has come to the Middle East to earn himself a fast buck, as our friends the Americans would say. You're a talented girl. Don't go wasting those talents on a man who might be good-looking enough, but have little beyond those looks. It doesn't pay.'

'It sounds like good advice,' said Dorna, mildly. In fact, she hardly knew what to say.

'So I shall give you plenty of time off,' said Hilary, briskly.

'Wait just one moment,' said Dorna, holding up her hand. 'I think we must sort something out, and that is the matter of expenses. I wish to pay my own.'

'That is entirely unnecessary,' said Hilary, firmly. 'When it comes to our contracts for the book, that will be another matter, but meanwhile I have decided that I want to work in Egypt and I have hired you ... well, perhaps "hired" is not quite the right word ...'

'It isn't,' said Dorna, firmly. 'I want to pay for myself.'

'But that is not sensible. Expenses can be quite heavy, and if I foot the bill, I can ask you to do little things for me in return. Surely that is a simple matter. I don't understand your objection, Dorna.'

Dorna hardly understood it herself, but she

only knew that she wanted to keep her own independence at all costs. She did not want to be beholden to Hilary Grant. She wished she had discussed this a little more with Liz Paige who had always been such a good friend to her. She wished she knew what was the regular thing to do. Liz had recommended the job to her, but sometimes Dorna had wondered if there had been a slight uneasiness in Liz's manner. Later she thought she knew the answer. It was because of what had happened with Mark. Liz had been afraid that Mark would turn up again and that she would let Hilary down at the last moment. That had surely been Liz Paige's prime concern.

But suppose it had not? Suppose she had wanted to warn Dorna that Hilary was not always the easiest of people to live with?

Yet who was? wondered Dorna, rather wearily. She must be difficult herself at times and she hated being disturbed by the telephone or the doorbell just when she was drawing in something very intricate which required care and concentration. She had been known to kick the leg of her drawing table if she got it wrong!

Now she debated with herself. Ought she to insist on her independence? Hilary was gathering her things together.

'Let's leave it for now,' she said, briskly. 'The time for argument is when I pay the bill.'

'The fares must be included.'

'Very well, the fares will be included.'

Dorna relaxed and smiled. Postponing a final decision meant that Hilary, too, would be given time to consider her position. But she did not want to be Hilary Grant's maid-of-all-work. She was an artist, not a hired servant.

'Where are we going this afternoon?' she asked. 'I shall hire a car,' said Hilary, 'and we will drive into Cairo. I think I would like to visit the Mameluke Mosque, and you will certainly be needed for that. Perhaps I ought to take pictures. I learned how to do it myself, instead of having to put up with impertinent girls who think they have wonderful talent.'

'Photography is not easy,' said Dorna.

'I'm aware of that. Haven't I just told you I have taken it up myself?'

Dorna made sure that her equipment was in good order, then she followed Hilary to their hired car.

CHAPTER SEVEN

Once again their car driver braved the heavy traffic of Cairo and Dorna stared out at the busy scene though it was the people who held her attention. They were beautiful people, she thought, even those who were old and those whose faces had been marked by suffering. She looked at elderly men wearing white beards and turbans, young men with noble heads, young women with great sad eyes and women who were hidden behind their black robes. Would they wear bright colours when they were within the confines of their own homes? she wondered. Would they laugh and make jokes, and play with their children?

When they reached the Citadel of Saladin, however, Dorna was once again awed by the majesty of Man's creation in Egypt.

'The view from here,' Hilary declared, 'must be one of the most famous in the world. You can see Cairo, with its domes and minarets, then the desert and the Giza Pyramids and a glimmering of the Nile.'

'I can't do justice to all of this,' said Dorna.

'I've got photographs,' said Hilary. 'Come and we'll go into the mosques.'

They walked towards an outer courtyard of the mosques where Dorna and Hilary removed their shoes and put on cloth slippers.

'It's strange,' said Hilary, 'that Saladin gave Cairo the great Citadel and surrounded the city by a wall with long stretches in the Citadel area but he did not live to dwell in the Citadel. It was not finished until his nephew, el-Kamil was king.'

'There must be a lesson in that somewhere for us,' said Dorna, thinking about Simon who always insisted that they should never waste a minute of their time.

They had passed through a room made

beautiful with paintings, stonework and woodwork and as they reached a trap door in the cement block floor, Hilary turned to Dorna.

'This leads to a burial vault,' she said. 'When a Moslem dies, the relatives go to the house, wrap the body in four or five layers of linen, put it in the coffin and carry it through the trap door to the tomb. The corpse is then taken from the coffin, introduced to the tomb then laid in the sand to return to the earth.'

Dorna shivered. Sometimes it seemed to her that in Egypt there was more preoccupation with the dead than the living.

'We can get a contrast now,' Hilary was saying, cheerfully. 'We'll go to the tomb of Mohammed Ali who died in 1849 ... his dynasty came down to Farouk, you know.'

'Do we have to?' Dorna asked.

Hilary stared. 'Of course we have to,' she said, impatiently. 'Don't tell me you're claustrophobic or something. You should not have accepted this commission if you are claustrophobic.'

'I'm not,' said Dorna. 'It's just that ... well ... that...'

She wondered how to explain that she was finding tombs rather depressing, though the fault might be in her and not in what they were trying to see and do. Nor could she understand the reason for her depression. She would have enjoyed it all so much more if Simon Elliott had brought her, she acknowledged to herself, as she forced herself to be honest. She could almost feel the warmth of his hand on her arm, a warmth which flowed straight to her heart. She could feel again the firm strength of his lips on hers and she knew that he had kindled something in her which would be part of her for always. Yet she so much wanted her independence. She wanted to do well with this work for Hilary Grant. It would be a stepping stone to other work and Dorna very much wanted to make a success of her career. She did not want, ever again, to be dependent on someone else, either economically or emotionally, which was why she had to get to know Simon Elliott a little better and to come to terms with this powerful attraction she felt for him. She must be able to cope with it. She was a free woman and well able to take care of herself, and perhaps that was why she wanted to pay every penny of her own expenses on this project.

'I was only thinking that tombs could be quite depressing,' said Dorna.

Hilary raised her eyebrows. 'You will just have to be depressed then, my dear, because a great deal of my book will feature these tombs. But I doubt if you'll find the Mosque of Mohammed Ali as depressing as all that.'

It was beautiful. Dorna paid for her own little slippers which had to be worn when they entered the Mosque. This time the white pillars, hanging lamps and Persian rugs in quiet shades of green delighted her eyes.

'Why, it's truly beautiful,' she said, softly.

'That high porch from which the Koran was read apparently did not lend itself to good acoustics and King Farouk gave that other set of steps, mostly in gold, so that the reading place could be changed.'

'Is it only the men who sit in prayer on the Persian rugs?' asked Dorna.

'Quite right. The women sit up in the balcony.'

'I should hate to live like that,' said Dorna. 'I like my independence.'

'Then your career is important to you.'

'Very important.'

'I thought so. Well, I *do* have influence, my dear,' said Hilary. 'We will have to see how well we work together, won't we?'

Her tone was gentle, but Dorna had the strange feeling that there was a warning for her somewhere. How much influence did Hilary really have, with regard to her work?

'We still have time to spare before dinner,' said Hilary. 'We could go on to the Museum for a preliminary visit. We could spend a week there if we became absorbed with the place, but that is not really my intention. But I think I shall have to do something on Tutankhamen. Perhaps we can leave that for another day.'

'No, I'd like to see some of that today,' said Dorna. 'I mean it will be a tremendous task to sketch even a few of the treasures.'

There was a special guard of soldiers around the glass cases which housed most of the wonderful treasure which Howard Carter removed from the tomb of King Tutankhamen.

Down the centre of the room were the four gold boxes with slanting sides which had fitted over the coffins and Dorna's teeth caught her lip as she sketched furiously.

'These are a "must",' she said. 'They are absolutely huge, though. You'll need to give proportions, Hilary, with these drawings.'

The second coffin was made of gold encrusted with precious stones, and the jewellery looked as new as any to be found in Bond Street.

'I adore the jewellery,' said Dorna.

'And I find these household things enchanting,' said Hilary. 'Just look at that umbrella used by the bearers to cover the King, and those leather gloves, and little figures of the household servants. And that bouquet of flowers ... brown, of course, but you can still see its shape. Thousands of years old, Dorna.'

'I know,' said Dorna, her eyes almost bemused. She was concentrating on the chariots and throne chairs.

'And grain ... which will grow today. It's been tried. I must make a point of writing about that,' said Hilary.

Suddenly she and Dorna turned to look at

one another and this time there was satisfaction between them. Dorna sighed with relief. She had been having strangely uneasy feelings about Hilary, that she might have made a mistake in coming to Egypt with her. She had begun to feel, instinctively, that they would not get on at all, as time went on. But now there was rapport between them once more.

'Should we venture into the "mummies room"?' asked Hilary, 'then we can return to the hotel.'

'Why not?' asked Dorna.

Her interest had been caught again by the beauty of the treasures she had seen. Perhaps they reached far into the past, but how absorbingly interesting they were in this present day, and how much beauty they had to offer. They were a feast for her eyes.

They had to buy a special ticket in order to visit the room which contained all the mummies of kings long-since dead.

'The guides do not like to go in there,' said Hilary. 'They're a superstitious lot. I hope you are not going to feel ... ah ... depressed again, Dorna?'

She laughed a little. Nevertheless Dorna felt that the place had a powerful effect on her. Row upon row of mummies, all in wooden coffins, had been stretched out, head to foot, along the room and Dorna walked up one row and down the other. They were all named and she paused for a moment before the mummy of Rameses II. He looked very thin and not too tall, and Dorna looked with compassion on the little leather figure who was sleeping with, what appeared to her, a smile on his face. He had been buried with luxury and now he shared a room with other pharoahs who had also prepared well for their after-life; a queen with glass eyes and hair braided in many small braids and a warrior pharoah who had fallen in battle and whose head had been wounded by an axe.

'It is sad to see them all like this,' she said to Hilary.

'Vanity, all is vanity,' Hilary murmured. 'Perhaps we ought to spend some time tomorrow, Dorna, assessing what we have got.'

'I agree with that,' Dorna told her. 'I shall have to work on a lot of these when I get back to my studio.'

'I hope you will give it all first priority,' said Hilary, sharply. 'I don't want to have my work set aside while you take on other commissions.'

'I wouldn't dream of it,' said Dorna. Really, Hilary did irritate her at times!

'Perhaps we shall see Simon Elliott when we get back to the hotel,' Hilary went on. 'I shall invite him to join us for dinner.'

'He might very well have his own plans,' Dorna put in. The thought stirred her with excitement that she might be seeing him again, but what if Hilary needled her into making some sort of indiscreet remark?

There was no sign of Simon at the hotel when they returned and Hilary insisted that they be served tea and biscuits at a small table near the window.

'I like tea at this time,' she said, grandly. 'Besides, we will see Mr Elliott if he should return soon. I'm really most interested in his television work. I would like to talk to him about it, and perhaps he will advise me on contacts. He must have good contacts.' She sipped her tea thoughtfully. 'They must work very far ahead when he is even considering a programme on the university for 1988.'

'I don't think he said that,' said Dorna. 'He said it was only preliminary ideas. Something in the pipeline.'

'You must make him understand that we are very interested,' said Hilary. 'If they start publicizing such an event, it may make my book quite topical.'

'I'm sure it will be well received,' said Dorna.

'I expect it will, as have the others,' said Hilary, 'but I want it to be more than that. I would like a best-seller,' said Hilary with a gleam in her eyes which caught Dorna's attention. 'Other people who write adventure books have their books featured much better than mine. Don't think I haven't noticed. This time I want mine to be well publicized.' She sighed deeply. 'I wonder how many more I shall write. I'm getting older now, you see, Dorna. I want success, *real* success. I wish I could make you understand.'

Dorna nodded. She did understand, but she was surprised by how much Hilary wanted that sort of success. Surely she ought to be content with what she had already.

'Lots of people would envy the success you have had,' she said, and Hilary sighed.

'I wonder how long I will be remembered after I am dead.'

Suddenly Dorna was laughing. 'I told you it was depressing to look at so many tombs,' she said. Dorna worked steadily in her room for the next hour, then she had a shower and changed into a simple filmy black gown with a sparkling lurex design on the close-fitting bodice. She touched her face delicately with make-up and brushed out her lovely honey-gold hair, then lightly touched her wrists with her best perfume before following Hilary downstairs to the diningroom. She was conscious that she looked her best, and Hilary smiled with approval when she saw her.

'You're a very striking young woman, Dorna,' she said admiringly. 'You must have had many admirers.'

Dorna smiled. 'I remember a certain interview we had when you preferred me to discourage admirers.'

'I told you. I'm a bad-tempered old woman at times.'

Her eyes swept the diningroom for Simon Elliott, then she paused abruptly. He was already there at a table in a secluded corner, talking earnestly to a girl wearing a dark crimson dress, whose dark hair was swept into a chignon at the back of her neck.

Dorna recognized the girl who had been with Simon at the airport, but she was unprepared for the sick jealousy which bubbled up within her, irrationally and almost unbelievably. How stupid to be jealous of an unknown girl! And even more stupid to be jealous of someone who was interested in Simon Elliott. He had every right to entertain whoever he wished. He had only kissed Dorna to amuse himself and he had no doubt expected her to be adult enough to accept his kisses in the same vein.

It was Hilary who had been urging her to invite his interest and she had imagined all the rest. She had imagined she would be able to attract him further, and perhaps get to know him better.

Now Dorna's cheeks flushed. She felt embarrassed by her own efforts in dressing up to attract a man.

'So our Mr Elliott has a lady companion,' said Hilary after they were shown to their table. 'He has not even noticed us.'

'She is part of his team,' said Dorna. 'I saw them together at the airport.'

Hilary was staring at them and Dorna felt

embarrassed. She only wanted to eat her meal, then disappear back upstairs and get on with her work. After all, she had come here primarily to work, not to enjoy herself.

But there did not seem to be much danger of that happening, she thought morosely, as she again glanced towards the well-shaped head with the curly brown hair which belonged to Simon Elliott. She noticed that his handsome looks attracted other admiring glances, but did not know that many of them were cast in her own direction.

'Perhaps he and his companion would like to join our table for dinner,' Hilary remarked hopefully.

Dorna stared. 'Oh, I shouldn't think so,' she said, shaking her head.

'Why don't you go and ask them?'

'I wouldn't *dream* of it,' she said, appalled by Hilary's lack of perception.

'If she is part of his team, then it won't be a romantic attachment. Why should they not join us?'

'How do you know it is *not* a romantic attachment? She is a very beautiful girl, and they are alone together. I would never butt in on them. It would be very bad manners.'

'You won't get very far, Dorna, if you're so reticent about making chances for yourself. I have heard it on good authority that it is a good idea to try to find a bit of influence if one wants to break into television. I am quite sure that Mr

Elliott has influence. He has that sort of air about him and I know he is interested in us. I could feel it.'

'And I think talent is needed most of all.'

'Of course you need talent, girl, but you need more than that. You need a bit of luck as well, and to be at the right place at the right time. I think we've had that sort of luck, finding Mr Elliott here in Cairo.'

'I don't think it will make any difference at all.'

Dorna spoke quickly, hoping to head Hilary off from interrupting Simon Elliott's dinner party. She did not want to talk to him or to break in on his *tête-à-tête* with the lovely girl in the dark crimson dress. If only there was some way she, herself, could get out of the diningroom without making a scene with Hilary, she would do it.

Also, she was beginning to stir with anger against Simon Elliott. He had kissed her and tried to pretend he was attracted to her. How dare he amuse himself at her expense! He and the girl were talking with absorption, to the exclusion of everyone else, and she could only conclude that their relationship was very close.

Then she took hold of herself. He might begin to notice her interest in them, and she must never allow him to suspect how much she minded, and how much his kisses had stirred her. Mark had sometimes complained that she was cold, but Dorna now knew herself to be capable of very deep desires and passions. She had never felt this almost unreasoning attraction for a man before, and it was going to need all the strength she had in her in order to keep her own integrity. She felt ashamed of her own needs.

And Hilary Grant was no help! It might have been difficult for her if Hilary had been against any contact with Simon Elliott. But the fact that Hilary was actively encouraging friendship between them seemed to make everything a great deal worse. Dorna had no wish to be thrown at his head.

'We all make our own luck,' Hilary was saying. 'I don't see why you cannot go over, on a friendly basis, and ask them to join us for coffee at least.'

'I refuse,' said Dorna clearly, 'and if you persist, Hilary, I shall go to my room. I shall get up and leave the diningroom right now.'

'You are a very foolish girl,' said Hilary, coldly. 'We are not getting on at all. I don't like your manner to me. Young girls of today are very impertinent to their elders.'

'I am here to do a job,' said Dorna, quietly. 'We agreed on that. I intend to do it, and I'm sure that you will find my work satisfactory. Now, if you don't mind ...'

She broke off, aware that Simon's tall figure was approaching their table and that his girl companion was walking out of the diningroom.

'Well, here you are,' he said. 'I thought you had changed your minds and had gone to eat in one of Cairo's best restaurants.'

'We arrived a little while ago, but you were otherwise engaged,' said Dorna, her eyes flickering towards the disappearing figure of the girl. Hilary Grant had put her into a very bad temper.

'Business,' he said, easily. 'We did not manage to finish all we wished to do this afternoon, but it is now concluded.'

'Does that mean you are returning to London?' asked Hilary with such obvious disappointment that Dorna felt embarrassed all over again. She had welcomed him with the warmest smile Dorna had ever seen on Hilary's lips.

'No, not quite yet. I ... ah ...' His gaze flickered over Dorna. 'I thought I might enjoy a day or two seeing the sights. I'm rather fond of Egypt and I find the Egyptian people delightful.'

Again he looked at her and she could feel the warm colour in her cheeks as he murmured the last word. Yet she knew she was behaving stupidly. It was sheer madness to allow this man to get such a hold of her heart. Or her senses. Was it only her senses? Was this overwhelming attraction for this man merely sexual? She had rarely felt sexual attraction towards any man with the possible exception of Mark and that had never been very strong.

Perhaps, if it had, she might now be looking forward to her wedding with Mark instead of losing him to another girl.

Yet she could think of that without any pain whatsoever. Perhaps her love had never gone very deep before, but she could not help being disturbed in every way by Simon Elliott. She glanced up at him and his golden-brown eyes smiled into hers so that her heart leapt, then pounded uncontrollably.

Casually he slipped into a chair at their table.

'I shall join you for coffee.'

'How splendid,' said Hilary. 'You are most welcome, Mr Elliott.'

'Simon will do.'

'Simon. I'm sure Dorna and I would be most interested in hearing all about behind the scenes, as it were, in the television studios. I expect a great deal is decided behind the scenes.'

'A great deal,' he agreed, his eyes on Dorna.

'And are you all talent scouts for your television companies? I mean, are you always on the lookout for new ideas, and new material?'

He turned to Hilary, then back to Dorna, his eyes dancing with mischief.

'Have we here a budding belly dancer?' he asked. 'I like watching old films on television where the heroine always managed to display her skills before the right talent scout, or the right producer, at the best possible moment. Orchestras would play out of sight and the whole performance would be so professional that the bemused producer could only applaud and offer the contract he carried in his inside pocket. Have you ever watched such films, Dorna?'

'No,' she said, shortly.

Her cheeks were still warm with colour and she knew that his eyes searched her face even though she had turned away.

'I'm sure Miss Grant knows exactly what I mean.'

'I do indeed. I used to enjoy such films myself though I rarely go to the cinema these days.'

'Well, you have quite a following for your books, mainly young adults I would expect.'

'And children, though my new book will be for the older children. Come to think of it, Simon, it *might* make a good television programme.'

Hilary trotted this out as though it were an idea newly born, and Simon's brows rose and his amber eyes rested on her thoughtfully, then he turned again to Dorna.

'We must think about that some time. I shall need more information, of course.' His voice was cool.

'I'm sure Dorna can supply all the information possible. We are both working on the book. If I might explain, it contrasts Ancient Egypt with the new, and also portrays

81

life as it is lived today. I think that is very important. Dorna could confirm that is so.'

'Good. Then you don't mind if I borrow her now and again, Miss Grant?'

'Not at all. I'm sure she will be quite safe in your hands, Simon.'

Dorna stared from one to the other, her eyes darkening. She felt like a parcel, ready to be passed round.

'I may not have the time,' she said, clearly. 'I have a lot of work to do on my drawings. I may wish to check up on things I might have missed and I must do that while we are still here. I can only find out if I work on them a little more.'

'There will be plenty of time for that, I'm quite sure,' said Hilary. 'Are you working here with a team then, Simon?'

'Yes, there are others. We are researching for a Middle East documentary. The other project is merely exploratory, with an eye to the future. Television is going to grow, you know, with many more channels requiring good programmes.'

'How exciting,' said Hilary. 'How very interesting you make it sound. Oh dear, I wonder if you two young people would excuse me. I'm an older woman now, and my digestion is not what it used to be. I'm always tempted to eat more at the dinner table than is good for me. Now I feel I would like to retire early.'

'I'll come with you,' said Dorna, beginning

to push back her chair.

'Oh no, my dear, I wouldn't dream of disturbing you. You must stay here and entertain Simon. Have more coffee. I'll say goodnight now, Dorna, and I shall see you both tomorrow.'

She excused herself and made a beeline for the elevator before Dorna had time to recover her breath.

Then Simon was leaning forward and was looking deep into her eyes.

'I had hoped to get rid of her later,' he said, 'but I didn't think it would be so easy.'

'You can get rid of me just as easily,' she said, this time standing up and reaching for her bag.

'But I don't want to be rid of you,' he said, softly. 'Sit down. I have a lot I wish to talk to you about.'

'I have work to do. I told you.'

'Not at this time, surely, and not in that dress. That would be a waste, Dorna.'

'If you want a companion, then why did you not remain with your friend in the dark red dress.'

'Sylvia? Her name is Sylvia Parrish. Let's go dancing, Dorna. The night is still young and it's a pity to waste an hour of it.'

'The night is no longer young, if you look properly at the time. We spent rather a lot of time talking after dinner, and that was late enough. I have to get up early in the morning.'

They had moved towards the elevator which they now saw was out of order once again. Dorna turned towards the stairs.

'I'm sorry,' she said, clearly, 'but I'll really have to say goodnight. I'm going up to my room.'

Her knees almost trembled as she started to climb the stairs and he fell into step beside her, then put a hand under her arm.

'I'll see you to your room then.'

'I . . . I wish you would leave me alone.' Her heart was beating twice as fast as usual and she was aware of nothing except his nearness.

'Do you, Dorna?' he was asking, softly.

He took the key of her room from her fingers and opened the door, then followed her inside.

'No,' she said, almost desperately. 'This is where I say goodnight.'

'Then say it properly,' he told her, and a moment later she was in his arms and she felt the strength of his firm lips on her own.

Dorna's body began to shake. No man had ever made her feel so completely helpless in his presence. She had no power to resist him. It was as though Simon Elliott had put a spell on her, and she could only cling to him as he held her in his arms.

'Oh Dorna,' he whispered. 'You're a very lovely girl.'

Again his lips claimed hers and she could feel his hands caressing her body so that she seemed to be on fire all over and there was a great clamouring tumult within her for the love of this man.

Then the thought of Sylvia Parrish came back to haunt her and, with a tremendous effort, she pushed him away.

'Please go,' she said, shakily. 'You might as well know that I don't sleep around.'

'I believe you.'

His golden eyes held hers and he reached up to stroke the damp hair off her forehead.

'What about special cases?'

'There *are* no special cases.'

Again he stared at her, then followed the smooth lines of her cheek and chin with one finger.

'Aren't there? Maybe it's too soon yet, but I hope I'm going to be a special case.'

He sighed and some of the tension went out of her.

'How is your project working out?' he asked. 'Are you managing to work well with Hilary Grant? Is she ... well ... easy to work with?'

'We get along okay. Why do you ask?'

'If you need me at any time for whatever reason, call me.' He gave her his room number. 'Where are you going tomorrow?'

'I'm not sure.' She was still shivering a little, but this normal conversation was beginning to have a steadying effect on her, and she wondered if Simon was doing it deliberately. She knew enough about men to know that he desired her and that he could so easily have forced the issue.

'We might go to the Valley of the Kings, perhaps. Hilary has already done some work on Egypt from previous visits, but I still have my drawings to do.'

He grinned and stroked his chin. 'She wants a television programme, doesn't she?'

'She does.'

'And she's bullying you into softening me up. Perhaps she realizes that it would not take much softening where *you* are concerned.'

Dorna's cheeks flamed. 'I have no desire at all to soften you up. How can you say such a thing?'

'Because it's the truth, of course. Isn't it?'

'I think you'd better go, Simon. I've had quite enough for one day.'

He grinned. 'Tell Hilary Grant that you've got a great deal more softening to do, and must spend as many hours as possible in my company.'

'Oh! ... you!,' she said, her eyes now sparkling with angry tears. He had disturbed her so much emotionally and now she could see that this was his way of answering Hilary. He had seen through her miles away, and had seen that Dorna was being thrown at his head as bait for a television programme.

He would have enjoyed making use of the bait if she had not resisted, and now he was returning her to Hilary with his message. He wanted more! Well, she was very tired of being used whether by Hilary or by Simon Elliott.

'Goodnight,' she said, furiously. 'I'm not here as entertainment for you, or ... or to be used as bait. I'm here to work.'

Again he caught her to him but this time she did her best to struggle free of him until she grew tired and remained quiet in his arms. He kissed her gently then, as he was about to let her go, he kissed her again with deep passion.

'Don't forget to call me if you need me ... for anything,' he added, rather thickly. Then the light of laughter returned to his eyes. 'And I do mean anything.'

'I don't need anyone except myself,' she told him. 'I can take care of my own affairs.'

He held her chin again between his finger and thumb, and now she saw that he was looking at her seriously, his eyes searching and probing.

'I think you may be right, Dorna,' he agreed. 'You are tougher than you appear at first glance. Don't go into huffs. I'm staying on in Egypt for a few days to have a break from dull routine. Let's enjoy it, you and I. Hilary will give you time off to keep softening me up. Don't tell her I'm on to her. That would spoil things.'

'I'm here to work!' she repeated. 'I'm not here on holiday and, even if I were, I wouldn't be spending my time with you. You already have ... have friends.'

'Now you're pretending to yourself,' he told

her. 'You know very well you want to be with me. You know I can reach you where it matters if only you would flatten down all these bristles.'

Again he touched her cheek lightly with his fingers so that she shivered.

'But I respect your wishes. In fact, I respect *you*, my dear. I will only stay when *you* want me to stay. You're afraid of yourself and your own feelings as yet. I can see it in your eyes. But we'll put that right as you get to know me a little better. Goodnight, my dear. I'll look out for you tomorrow.'

She said nothing and he lightly kissed the top of her head then slipped from the room. Slowly she walked over to her chair beside the window and sat down as though her legs would no longer support her. Looking out of the window, once again she saw the wonderful, romantic view of the pyramids and suddenly her heart surged with feeling and her whole instinct was to rush to the telephone and call Simon's room number, asking for him to come back. Her whole body clamoured for his love.

Then after a time she managed to find her commonsense once more. He was a stranger, this man who had come into her life, but if she were not careful, he was going to disrupt her whole life. She must remember, every moment, why she had come to Egypt in the first place. She must not allow a strange man to put her off-course.

Yet her heart said he was not a stranger. He could so easily be part of her, if she let him. She wanted him. She wanted him more than she had ever wanted a man, but he was hardly likely to have much respect for her if she gave in to such feelings. He might make love to her, but he would not respect her afterwards. As far as he was concerned, she was only bait for Hilary to dangle in front of him, and the fish had looked at the fly and had spotted the hook!

Dorna's cheeks were hot with humiliation. She wished the project finished now so that she could get back home to London. She wanted to be free of it all.

CHAPTER EIGHT

The following morning Hilary's mood had changed once more, and changed quite dramatically. Dorna suspected that she had been perceptive enough to see that Simon Elliott had seen through her manoeuvres to interest him in a possible television series, and she was now feeling angered and embarrassed.

'I have changed my mind about Mr Elliott,' she said, without preamble. 'He can go his own way. There is no need to encourage him, Dorna.'

'Why? What has happened?'

In spite of all her good resolutions, Dorna's

heart sank with dismay.

'I've remembered where I saw him before,' said Hilary. 'He's not really the man of influence I had believed him to be.'

Dorna stared. 'Where?' she asked. 'Where have you seen him before?'

'I've just told you. It was of no importance whatsoever. He is not anyone special. Now have you any shopping you want to do in Cairo? We could take a taxi in order to do any shopping we need, then I suggest that we move on to Luxor. I shall book a flight for us and a hotel I know at Luxor...'

'Oh, no!' said Dorna, involuntarily.

She had not seen Simon that morning but she would feel very badly indeed if she checked out of the hotel without a word to him, and without telling him that she had travelled on to Luxor. If she left now, it was highly unlikely that they would ever see one another again, and her instinctive reaction was one of dismay, and a blind desire to see Simon straight away. It was mad and senseless, but she could not help herself.

'What's the matter with you, girl?' Hilary was asking, crossly. 'I thought you had no interest in this man. As a matter of fact, I have to acknowledge that you were a better judge of him than I. I should have respected your feelings and I am sorry.'

Really, thought Dorna, she was the most changeable person she had ever known, though it also seemed that she must know something which was not to Simon's credit.

'Is he a criminal or ... or something?' she asked, half-fearfully.

'No, of course not. He's just ... just very ordinary, that's all.'

'Then I would not like to leave so suddenly without saying goodbye to Mr Elliott,' Dorna insisted. 'I mean, it would be rather rude, wouldn't it?'

'No it would not. He is not part of our team. Presumably he has his own work to do, *and* he has his own friends. Surely you cannot be forming a romantic attachment for the man when you were made well aware that he already had a woman with him? And it is only a comparatively short time since you were engaged to marry some other young man.'

Dorna's face flushed.

'Miss Parrish is a colleague of Simon's,' she said, then she wished she had held her tongue when Hilary's dark eyes stared at her balefully.

'And to her, you are no doubt a good contact for his research work. If you must know, I did enquire about our Mr Elliott this morning. I wanted to satisfy myself that I was not mistaken and that I had met him before, or ... or seen him before at any rate. But I was informed that he had left the hotel with Miss ... ah ... Parrish. They did not know when he was expected back.'

Dorna's heart jerked, then she felt almost

sick with disappointment. His last words to her had been that he would see her this morning, yet already he had left the hotel with Sylvia Parrish. *Was* she a colleague? Simon had said very little about her.

She had lost him, Dorna thought, by being too cautious. Now that he had gone, regrets were setting in even though she knew it was better this way. But she still wanted him and she had been afraid to allow herself to become involved with him. She had been afraid of being hurt again. Now Dorna felt an almost unbearable sense of loss, though her commonsense kept telling her that she should be glad it was all over. The most sensible thing to do was to agree with Hilary Grant that they should move on, and for her to forget Simon Elliott. He was a man who had touched her life and had left a memory which would probably be with her always, but she must forget about him if she were to make a success of life on her own. Presently Hilary would no doubt tell her all she knew about Simon, though at the moment she was strangely reluctant to listen. She did not want to hear anything to his detriment.

'Pack up your things, Dorna,' said Hilary as she came back from the reception desk. 'We move on to Luxor. I've booked seats on the plane leaving at 12 noon, and I have obtained two rooms for us at the Hotel Etap Luxor. We can do any shopping we wish in Cairo and we can have tea and toast at the Hilton before we leave. I'll arrange transport.'

'I will settle my own bill,' Dorna insisted.

'As you wish,' said Hilary, indifferently, 'though I find this great desire for independence rather boring.'

'I want to be free to make my own decisions,' said Dorna firmly, 'and I don't want to be a paid companion, that's all.'

'Decisions? Such as staying behind here for the sake of spending another hour in the company of Simon Elliott. How will that benefit you, Dorna? If you think he plans to form some sort of ... ah ... attachment to you, I hope you will not be disappointed when you find out otherwise. I made a mistake encouraging you to be friends with him. I want to right that mistake.'

Dorna looked into Hilary's dark eyes. Her face could look almost cruel at times.

'Do you really know something to his detriment?' she asked.

'It was a personal matter, that's all, but I would not want to see you hurt.'

Dorna considered, then she nodded. 'I shan't stay behind,' she said, quietly. 'I know you wish to do more work at the Valley of the Kings, and I must confess that I am eager to work there myself. It won't take me very long to pack.'

Nevertheless she wished, deep in her heart, that Simon would return before they checked out! Surely it would be a matter of courtesy for her to say goodbye formally. She did not know where to find him in London, nor did he know her address.

Ought she to leave a note at the desk? Dorna deliberated, but already Hilary was impatient to leave and she had to settle her bill.

Then she followed Hilary to the waiting taxi.

*   *   *

The Hotel Etap Luxor was very up-to-date with a lovely sunken reception area, modern lounges and comfortable chairs. Dorna loved it on sight, even though her thoughts were still with Simon. Would she ever see him again?

Her room looked out on to a very busy road running along the Nile, and across the Nile lay the Valley of the Kings. In spite of her constant feeling of loss and disappointment, her spirits lifted and her heart beat faster with excitement. Egypt, she decided, was a wonderful country and she longed to start work again.

She was finding Hilary a difficult moody person to get along with, but no doubt Hilary thought the same way about her! They were both craftsmen, doing a rather lonely job, but where their work touched, Dorna enjoyed producing the drawing which Hilary needed and over which their interest could be equally captured.

But once again the travelling had tired

Hilary and she rested in her room.

'Don't bother me, Dorna,' she said crossly. 'I don't want to sit with you while you're sulking because you've left that young man behind in Cairo. I should have known better than to bring a young girl with me again. I should have remembered. They always want a man to be hovering somewhere in the background.'

Dorna's eyes glinted. 'I don't think that's quite fair, Hilary,' she said, quietly, 'and I would like to remind you that I'm here independently of you. If we can't get along together, I'm sure Liz Paige can find you a replacement...'

'That would ruin everything! We've gone too far for that!'

'Then you'll have to put up with me as I am,' said Dorna. 'And if you wonder why I want to pay my own expenses, then this is a prime example.'

'We did very well until Simon Elliott barged in,' said Hilary. 'He should mind his own business. I wonder...'

She grew very thoughtful and lapsed into silence.

'What?' Dorna asked.

'Oh ... nothing ... nothing. I can't decide whether or not he remembers me. I rather feel that he does and it might account for...' She stared almost unseeingly at Dorna. 'Yes, that might be why he made our acquaintance.'

'Where did you meet him?' Dorna asked, eaten up with curiosity. 'What do you know about him?'

'I don't know him at all. I met his wife, of course. Did you know he had been married? She was a silly little thing, very full of her own importance, and always wanting her own way. I had to be firm with her. I would not put up with her sort of behaviour.'

'What happened?' Dorna was all ears.

'Nothing of much importance from my point of view because we could not use much of her stuff. She took photographs, you know, and tried to pretend it was very skilful.'

'But it *is* skilful if you want to be good,' Dorna said, mildly.

'Not as much as *she* pretended.'

'Where is she now?' Dorna asked.

Hilary sighed a little. 'Well, it was rather sad later. She died of an overdose of drugs, or something. That's where I saw Simon Elliott … at the funeral. I did not know him and she worked under her maiden name. But I felt I owed it to the girl to go to the funeral. I doubt if he would notice me there, but I remember him clearly now and I heard someone remark that he blamed some of the people she worked with for the tragedy … me included! Of course he was not a big TV man then … doing a bit of journalism, or some such thing. But if he really blamed me for not helping the girl when she was depressed, I hardly think he can do anything for me now. I'm undecided about television. I can always find someone else, of course. I *do* have influence, Dorna. Don't forget that.'

Dorna turned away, sighing. She was getting a little tired of Hilary's influence. If her book turned out well, it would sell. If not, then she could start thinking about the next one.

But how sad for Simon Elliott that his young wife had died because of an overdose of drugs, though she failed to see why he would ever blame Hilary ... unless she had been using that influence of hers against Mrs Elliott. No wonder he had not wanted to talk about it. Was that why he had never married again? No doubt he'd had plenty of affairs, though, and he might have worn down her defences if they had been together any longer. He was the most attractive man she had ever met.

But it was not in her nature to have affairs. She felt things too deeply, and Mark had hurt her very much. Even now she could feel hurt by his treatment of her when she thought about it.

Dorna sat out on her balcony feeling lonely and rather lost. London seemed to be very far away and she wondered if everything was going well with her cousin Alison at the flat. She had not seen much of Alison when she was growing up, but Aunt Claire was a sweet soul, full of good commonsense. No doubt Alison was very like her mother and would be looking after everything very well.

How vastly different London was from the scene now in front of her. She looked out at the many little horses and buggies with their native drivers, the drivers' robes flying around them, jingling bells and shouting encouragement. Donkeys, pulling other types of carts, lumbered along, their drivers sitting on produce piled high in the carts.

Across the Nile she could see a village where a Moslem was saying his prayers by the side of the river whilst far beyond she watched the beautiful orange sunset and her heart surged once more with the excitement of being here in this beautiful country. She was in Egypt and she loved it.

Outside four people climbed into one of the buggies in order to visit the Karnak Temple by night. The buggy was decorated like a Christmas tree, with silver tinsel, paper flowers and jingling bells.

Dorna watched them go, then she went back into her room and began to improve on the sketches she had made before going to the restaurant in search of food.

It had been a long day.

CHAPTER NINE

Next day Hilary declared herself well enough to make another visit to the temple.

'I have already seen it by night,' she told Dorna, 'and I have no wish to listen to another lecture on Rameses II accompanied by the sound of music and artificial lights. Perhaps it does stir the imagination, and people can more easily imagine the time when the temple was at the height of its glory and could only be entered by priests and kings.'

'It sounds wonderful,' said Dorna. 'Luxor is really exciting.'

'You will see it better in daylight. You can't sketch the place in the dark.'

It was a beautiful day and Dorna viewed the ancient temple against the deep blue of an Egyptian sky, and she forgot everything else as she sketched the wonderful carvings and paintings dedicated to the worship of the sun-God, Amon-Ra and examined the hieroglyphics of Ancient Egypt.

It was a huge temple built by Amenophis III and Rameses II.

'It was orginally 623 feet in length,' said Hilary, looking at her notes, 'but that great builder, Rameses II, added to it and by the time he had constructed that large colonnaded court in front of the completed temple, it grew to 853 feet!'

'Everything is so huge,' said Dorna, awed. 'It makes me feel so ... so insignificant somehow.'

'Wait until you see the Colossi of Rameses II.'

'There are so many statues of Rameses II,' said Dorna. 'He must have been very fond of having statues made of himself.'

'Alexander the Great reconstructed the Sanctuary of the Sacred Boat,' said Hilary. 'Pay particular attention to that, Dorna. Also there is a small temple dedicated by the Emperor Hadrian at the north-west corner of the enclosure.'

Dorna nodded. She was examining, with fascination, the carvings on the wall which recorded the greatness of Rameses II as he slew his enemies, held talks with his generals and took prisoners in battle. Here the king was shown standing on his enemies.

'I heartily approve of the man,' said Hilary. 'One must stand on one's enemies or they'll end up standing on you.'

Dorna laughed, then saw that Hilary was not in an amusing mood. She looked again at the wonderful statues of Rameses II and his favourite, Queen Nefertari, and thought again about Simon. If only he had been here to share all this wonder with her, how much more she might have enjoyed his companionship that that of Hilary Grant. She missed him acutely. She could not help herself.

'Do you want the obelisks given by the Queen Hatshepsut?' she asked Hilary as they moved onwards.

'Certainly.'

'There is so much, I shall have to take

photographs and tie them in with my sketches later.' She was silent as she worked. 'I wonder what happened to all those daughters of Rameses,' she mused, '107 daughters and 98 sons ... is that correct?'

'He married them,' said Hilary, briskly.

This time she managed to smile at Dorna's answering peal of laughter.

'Tomorrow we will go to the Temple of Hatshepsut. Very interesting that temple. The architect was her lover, you know. I've seen a little alcove there where he carved his name, brave fellow ... out of ordinary sight, but still there.'

That described Simon for her, thought Dorna. He was out of her sight, but somewhere in Cairo he was probably talking and laughing with Sylvia Parrish.

They left early next morning by boat for Thebes and after the tremendous heat of the previous day, Dorna welcomed the fresh breeze which was blowing on the water.

She loved looking at the colourful carts driven by natives on the road, and the equally colourful boats on the Nile. The sky was unbelievably blue and for a while her heart was at peace. Hilary, too, was in a better temper and not quite so hectoring in her manner towards Dorna. She certainly would hate to be her paid companion, however, thought Dorna. Hilary would turn any girl she employed into a slave. She could always find the right remark to undermine one's confidence, but Dorna was now an experienced craftswoman and she had managed to get through quite a lot of work.

But Hilary was well qualified to deal with the vendors they met on either side of the river as they left the boat and boarded a bus.

'We'll be besieged if we blink an eyelid,' she said, roundly. 'Into that bus, Dorna. We can buy anything we want in the villages. All these souvenirs are made there in any case.'

Dorna loved the villages which they drove through, and which reflected a wonderfully simple life so different from her own. Would she have been happy living such a life? She would no doubt have married some suitable man, learned how to make bread, borne children and gossiped with other women as she washed her laundry in the Nile. Yet everyone looked happy and content with their lot, whilst she ... she had lost her inner contentment. Now she felt restless and dissatisfied with her life.

'Deir-el-Bahri,' said Hilary at length, 'and the Temple of Hatshepsut. She was the pharoah's daughter who found Moses, you know, but you won't find mention of it here in Egypt.'

Dorna's interest sharpened immediately and as she looked up at the three terraces of the magnificent temple, all else was forgotten except a desire to get it all down on paper.

'Much of it has been restored by the

Americans,' Hilary told her. 'I have quite a few notes on the subject. When Queen Hatshepsut built the temple, it was the custom to separate the tomb and the temple because of grave robbers. However, the queen had her tomb hewn from the face of the cliff on the west face and her temple built on the east face. You can see this secretly restores the unity of the tomb and the temple. I have a great admiration for Queen Hatshepsut. She will figure largely in my book.'

'It's beautiful,' said Dorna, looking at the colonnades of square pillars in limestone in front of the terraces which had no doubt been part of the rebuilding project. The horizontal effect seemed to tower into the side of the mountain.

'It was more of a temple of worship to the God Amon of Thebes, than a funeral temple,' said Hilary. 'The God Amon assimilated the sun-God and became supreme God of Egypt, the salvation of both the living and the dead. We will walk up to the second terrace and you can look at the paintings, Dorna, but much has been destroyed deliberately.'

'Oh, how terrible,' said Dorna.

'It was done by her son-in-law, Tuthmosis III who hated her for the way she kept him under her in importance. In my opinion she was right to do so. When he succeeded her, he had her face carved out of all the paintings so that her Ka could not find her. One, in a dark corner, was left untouched. I would like to think deliberately so.'

Dorna worked at great speed. There was so much to see and do; Hatshepsut's mother on a birth chair surrounded by her maids, the queen as a child receiving milk from a sacred cow; a symbolic painting with Hatshepsut shown at one with the Gods by having a woman's body and the head of the sacred cow.

'Divine conception, you see,' said Hilary. 'She must be shown to be a God.'

'With all this, I might have believed in her divinity myself,' Dorna agreed.

The day was becoming increasingly hot and Dorna watched the small boys running happily in the burning sand which would have scorched her own feet, their small white shirts flying as they ran after the strangers in their land.

She sketched one youngster, delighting in his large beautiful eyes and bright smile, then she would have given him a coin if Hilary had not stopped her.

'I told you, no tips,' she said, crossly. 'Why don't you listen?'

'He's so sweet,' said Dorna, 'and I have made use of him.'

*   *   *

At the entrance of the Valley of the Kings, Dorna stared at the Colossi of Memnon, two huge statues each cut out of one piece of hard sandstone. They represented Amenophis III seated on a gigantic throne. The south colossus originally wore a crown and the north showed the king between his mother Mut-em-weye and his wife Teye.

'I think I am going to have to use my camera again,' said Dorna. 'This is marvellous but I need more time to do it justice.'

'Very well, but I *do* want accuracy. Illustrations are an important part of my book, as you should know. Really, I *would* prefer to employ you then I could dictate my terms so much better. I am not used to this independence of yours. I have to leave things to your judgement instead of insisting that you follow mine.'

Put like that, Dorna felt she could see Hilary's point of view. Why did she have this strange desire to be herself? Why did she feel so instinctively that she should not depend too much on Hilary?

Now she worked as fast as she was able, then they passed between the Colossi and looked beyond to the hills of sand. They walked through a ticket gate then walked onwards to the Tomb of Tutankhamen. It was fenced round with a stone wall and they passed through another gate where Dorna was obliged to leave her camera with a native.

'No photographs in *this* tomb,' said Hilary with a glint in her eyes.

Dorna smiled. 'You know I do *not* rely on my camera all the time. I would not be so valuable to you otherwise.'

They walked down a long ramp to the tomb and again Dorna felt disappointed that her companion was Hilary Grant and not Simon Elliott. Yet Hilary was an interesting companion who could give her quite a few gems of information which enhanced the wonder and excitement of all she was seeing in Egypt. But she had no doubt that Simon would have been equally well informed, and his very presence would have made the place a world of enchantment for her. If only . . .

'It's smaller than I imagined,' said Dorna, as they walked out of the tomb.

'Part of the tomb is sealed off,' said Hilary, briefly.

They walked from the ramp directly into a room without decoration which made Dorna think of the unfinished walls of a basement, and then turned to look at the end of the room. The walls were gorgeous. They continued up three steps to a platform from where they could see the burial room, and Dorna caught her breath at the sight of such beautiful paintings. What wonderful craftsmen they were! she thought. It was difficult to imagine that this work had been done thousands of years before.

'Funeral scenes,' Hilary was saying. 'Transporting the coffin on a sledge. Each king doing honour to his predecessor . . . the king and his Ka in front of Osiris.'

'What are those?' asked Dorna.

'Dog-headed Gods from the Amduat.'

In this innermost shrine was the rectangular stone sarcophagus and inside this, again protected by a sheet of glass, was the largest of the coffins with the mummified remains of King Tutankhamen inside. The smallest of the coffins was the one made of solid gold which Dorna had already seen in the Museum in Cairo.

'What splendour,' said Dorna, wonderingly, 'yet Tutankhamen was only eighteen when he died. I wonder what all those other tombs were like before they were plundered.'

'One can only assume they were even more wondrous,' said Hilary, as they wandered out once more into the heat of the day, then on to the tomb of Rameses VI.

'I can't help thinking they must have minded very much that their tombs were robbed and their remains disturbed like this,' said Dorna, shivering despite the heat. 'I find I cannot put my heart into doing justice to these drawings.'

'Such imagination!' Hilary scoffed. 'You speak as though their ghosts still lived on, peering over your shoulder.'

'Don't!' said Dorna.

'Stupid girl. How *can* you believe in such things? You are as superstitious as those misguided mortal creatures and perhaps you think that bad luck will now dog your footsteps and that your happiness and well-being will be torn from you? We have no time for such nonsense these days.'

Dorna's face had paled, and again she shivered. Perhaps she was stupid to be a prey to such imaginations, but she did not feel at all comfortable in these tombs.

'It was the tomb of Rameses VI which kept that of Tutankhamen intact over the centuries,' said Hilary. 'The entrance to this one is directly over that of Tutankhamen.'

This tomb had quite a different type of entrance from the previous one. As they walked through the iron gates, it looked like a long hall descending in a gradual decline. It was lighted by electricity and showed where the seven doors would originally have sealed the tomb.

The walls of the corridor were covered in beautiful paintings, depicting scenes from the life of Rameses and mainly executed in white, red, black with touches of yellow.

At the end of the long hallway, they entered a room which appeared to be supported by four huge pillars, and in the centre of the room had been placed a broken sarcophagus. On three sides, a few feet higher, were other rooms which would originally have held the funerary furniture, but it was the ceiling of this room which held Dorna's interest, even fascination. Scenes from the 'Book of Day and Night' had been painted in deep blue, the figures featured in gold. The preservation was wonderful and Dorna could only stare at it with wonder and fascination. She turned to the other walls in the tomb which depicted scenes from 'The Book of the Gates,' 'The Book of Caverns,' and 'The Book of the Dead'.

'I'm lost in wonder at the skill of it all,' said Dorna. 'It makes me feel very humble.'

'Well, you had better forget to be humble and turn in some good work,' said Hilary. 'There is a place called the "Rest House",' she added as they came out of the tomb. 'We can get something to drink there. Beer, perhaps.'

'I dislike beer,' said Dorna.

'Minerals then, unless you can do without anything. I can tell you now that the toilets are a disaster.'

Suddenly Dorna was laughing again. Sometimes Hilary, with her caustic remarks, could be good company. At other times her remarks could be more pointed and even hurtful. She was certainly not the easiest person to work with, and Dorna could never make up her mind whether she liked her or not. Sometimes Hilary seemed a bitter sort of woman, then she would glimpse a hint of loneliness behind that image and she would wonder a little. Had she been a young, happy girl once, a girl who had had a bad experience?

'I'll have some pop,' she said, 'but I could certainly do with a sit-down for a few minutes. My feet are beginning to kill me.'

'I would swap them for mine any day,' said Hilary ruefully. 'It's always a hazard for me.'

'Does it make you feel bad-tempered?' Dorna asked with an impish smile.

'Not at all,' said Hilary, equably. 'Incompetence makes me bad-tempered. We are about to besieged by vendors again. Don't buy anything, Dorna, it only encourages them and I see a group of soldiers over there who are watching carefully. They might turn nasty with the vendors if we encourage them in here, anyway.'

Dorna would have preferred to buy a few souvenirs, but she respected Hilary's knowledge and experience. It had grown very hot and Hilary debated with herself whether or not to go back to the hotel.

'There's a village I want to see,' she explained to Dorna. 'It's where all those antiques are made.'

'Antiques! Made!' echoed Dorna.

'Of course. They are fakes. Can't you see that? They are made in a village not far from here. It might provide some very good material though, there again, I already have quite a few notes.'

Dorna debated with herself for a moment. Hilary looked very hot and tired but she was feeling more refreshed after sitting in the porch. Hilary had drunk beer, but she'd had mineral water.

'I could perhaps join that bus for tourists,'

she suggested. 'You could take a car back to the hotel. If you tell me what you want particularly, I'll do the sketches and take photographs, and I can probably be back at the hotel for lunch. Where do we go after lunch?'

'Karnak. The Temple of Karnak again. I want more photographs and drawings of the flowering bushes by the sacred lake, and I want a drawing of the Scarab. You can walk round the Scarab and make a wish, if you like, though I don't promise it will come true!'

'Then I shall be careful not to depend on it,' said Dorna, gravely.

She saw Hilary into a car, then she joined the bus, sitting half-way up on the righthand side. There were a great many tourists in the bus which took off a short time later, and Dorna looked eagerly out of the window. She often felt awed and fascinated by all she saw in the tombs, but rural Egypt was a delight to her. Her eyes would follow the little paths winding upwards through the sandhills to the mud huts of the villages where women, dressed entirely in black, walked with stately carriage, balancing jugs on their shoulders. The children were practically naked though others wore every type of clothing and romped madly as they played together. Dorna knew that education was now compulsory in all the villages but she often wondered *when* the children went to school. It appeared to her that they had a great many holidays which they evidently enjoyed, though Hilary said they were still sent out, in isolated villages, to work in the fields.

Dorna had been so lost in thought that she was hardly aware that another passenger had slipped into the seat beside her. She was watching the animals, the dogs who always seemed to be beset by flies, and the small hardworking donkeys.

'Do you find it *so* absorbing?'

A voice spoke in her ear and Dorna's heart leapt, then raced wildly as she turned to stare into Simon Elliott's amused eyes.

'Simon! What are you doing here?'

'Some detective work in the best Hercule Poirot tradition. Since Agatha Christie's *Death on the Nile* I always associate this place with Hercule Poirot now.'

'But ... how?'

'Oh, I had to part with some "squeeze" back at the hotel, and a bit more when I got to Luxor, but I've tracked you down, my dear Dorna. I saw you and Hilary Grant parting company, and I saw her making off towards Luxor while you boarded the bus. So here I am! I thought I would wait quietly till we were on our way before making my presence known to you. I can only assume you're hiding from me, when you left no message at the hotel. I was not very happy about that, Dorna.'

She was getting her breath back.

'Hilary wanted us to be on our way immediately, and you *had* gone out with your friend, Miss Parrish.'

'*Mrs* Parrish,' he corrected.

'Oh.'

Did that make things better, or worse? She did not think that marriage ties would mean much to Simon Elliott, if he wanted his own way. Then a bubble of happiness began to form in her heart. What did it matter? It was a wonderful day and she was loving this beautiful country with its kind and fascinating people. She was loving every minute of it.

'So Miss Grant rumbled me,' Simon said.

'She said she remembered where she had seen you before.'

'I thought she would eventually. I notice she is no longer hanging on my every word, hoping I'll have some "influence" ... she's a great one on "influence" isn't she? ... to get her some television publicity.'

'Have you?'

'I might have. She's good enough, so she doesn't need to fawn all over me, though I expect that's all in the past now.'

Dorna was silent for a moment.

'What happened when she knew you before, Simon?' she asked, gently.

What happened about his wife? she wondered. If only he would tell her!

'I expect Miss Grant will tell you all about it sooner or later.' He sighed deeply. 'My wife worked for her at one time, that's all. My wife was a photographer. Now Miss Grant prefers

113

to work with an artist ... you! How is the work going, Dorna? Are you working well with her?'

'Oh ... quite well. Very well, maybe.'

She wanted to hear more. She wanted to know all about his wife. Hadn't she been given sufficient credit by Hilary for the work she had done? Hilary had said her work was not good enough, but that was only one side of it.

But somehow Simon was not the kind of person to be questioned when he put up his barriers. They were invisible but one was very much aware of them. She glanced up at him and her heart bounded again. How handsome he was! His skin was tanned to a rich golden colour, and his eyes were amber and flecked with gold as he turned to stare at her. The curls which clustered close to his head were clean and shining, as were his teeth as he smiled at her.

'I suppose Hilary told you about this village,' he said. 'This is where they manufacture "antiques". It's absolutely true. Come on and we'll have a look. We did a programme on it once. As a matter of fact, I remember it with great pleasure.'

In this village the houses were on a lower level than those they had already passed. Simon conducted Dorna into a building shaped like a 'T' with a type of verandah which appeared to consist of sticks supporting lengths of tin, over which palms were hanging, the whole designed to protect the workmen who sat outside, chiselling the articles which were on sale everywhere in Thebes. Dorna recognized many of the souvenirs she had wanted to buy from the vendors back at the tombs.

Her fingers itched for her pencil and pad as she looked at a workman, a huge grin on his face, squatting on the ground and behind him ranged his family who no doubt lived upstairs, since a narrow staircase was visible behind them. He was carving a sarcophagus with a tiny mummy inside whilst another carved a head of Nefertiti.

'This is marvellous,' said Dorna. 'I think I need a photograph as well.'

Presently they entered the building and looked over the many articles offered for sale, in very cramped quarters.

'If you want anything, you have to bargain them down,' said Simon.

'No, I don't want to bargain them down, and I do want a few things. I feel I owe it to them.'

'Then let me do it. I take it you want a sarcophagus and a head of Nefertiti since you appear to be absorbed by those.'

'Right. But you won't stop me buying some tiny carved beetles from the smallest children, poor little babies.'

'They will only despise you for being soft.'

'Perhaps. But I like to pay my debts.'

He looked at her curiously. 'I believe you do, Dorna. You are a very independent girl. I think you are very capable of looking after yourself and I should not worry about you.'

'*Worry* about me?'

He grinned. 'I'm a great worrier.'

Yet there had been a thoughtful note in his voice. Did he, perhaps, prefer helpless women? Had his wife given up her career after they married? Some men preferred it that way. But of course, she had not. Hilary had said she was married when she worked for her, but had used her maiden name. If only he would tell her about his wife...

But Dorna would never want to give up her career, though ... her thoughts raced on ... it was never likely that she would marry Simon Elliott! Yet he had an almost magnetic attraction for her, and her heart felt soothed and light as air now that he was with her again. It was as though the whole place had been swamped in golden light now that he was once again by her side.

She sighed a little as they sat on the bus to return to Luxor. She had enjoyed this trip with Simon so much. It had been such fun and so relaxing after some of her journeys with Hilary who was inclined to pluck at her arm and tell her to make sure she was including certain things among her drawings. Hilary always made her aware that she was working on this trip.

Yet now it was almost over. In another day or two she would be leaving Egypt for London, and now that Simon had found her again, she did not want to go! She only knew that she wanted this trip to last for ever ... if only he were by her side for the rest of the time.

'Why the great sigh?' he asked. 'Am I such boring company?'

'Oh no, nothing like that!'

She turned to him and felt the colour staining her cheeks.

'Where do you go from here?' he asked.

'Hilary wants to look at the Temple of Karnak again. After that...' she spread her hands, '... I expect we will have done enough for this particular book. She had material ready from her last trip, you see.'

'But there's so much more for you to see and enjoy! Why can't we go sight-seeing tomorrow? We can go to Aswan by bus and I guarantee you will love every minute of it.'

Dorna's heart beat faster with longing. What a wonderful day that would make! But Hilary would never hear of it. She would never allow Dorna to go off with Simon Elliott. She appeared to want to avoid Simon at all costs, and Dorna had the feeling that Hilary's temper could be quite ugly if she chose.

'What about your friend Mrs Parrish?' she asked.

'What about her? As far as I know, she plans to travel back to London and will be getting on with her work. She is part of our television research team, and she is very good.'

And her husband? Dorna wondered. What about her husband? Was she happily married or was she not above having an affair with Simon when they had to work together on projects which took them into fascinating countries like Egypt? She dug her nails into her palms and forced down the bitter taste of jealousy. She had never before experienced such an emotion. But never before had a man laid hold of her heart so completely, and in such a short time. She knew now that even if Simon had not found her so soon, she would not have rested until she had found him again! She wanted to feel his arms round her once more and she wanted his kisses. *How* she wanted his kisses!

'Are you afraid of Hilary Grant, Dorna?' Simon was asking, quietly. 'Is that your problem?'

'Afraid? No . . . not really. Well, perhaps I do feel I have to consider her first. After all, I would not be here if it were not for Hilary.'

'But she dominates you? She hasn't threatened you, I hope?'

His tone was casual, but he looked at her keenly.

'Threatened me? Oh no, nothing like that.'

But she would be scathing and sarcastic if Dorna declared that she wanted a day off to go sight-seeing with Simon. It would spoil the day.

'Sometimes she makes me feel angry,' she

admitted, 'then I feel sorry for her.'

'Sorry for her?'

'Yes. There's something rather sad about her. I think she must have been badly hurt at one time.'

'No reason for taking it out on other people,' said Simon. 'Well, here we are back at the landing stage. We take a boat now, across the Nile, and back to our hotel. Oh yes, I found it, and I am staying there, too. I've stayed there before and I find it very comfortable, and the food is excellent. This time I shall allow you to eat whatever you fancy. I think I will join you for dinner tonight.'

She bit her lip. Hilary would not like it! Then she remembered that she was independent of Hilary Grant. Why should she keep allowing the older woman to dictate to her?

'Well...'

'No need to mention to Miss Grant that I am here. I shall quietly join you at your table, and I hardly think she will make a scene. I can soon talk her into tolerating my company around the place. Tomorrow I intend to spend a happy day with you, Dorna. After all, I don't have many days when I am free of work.'

'But I am not free of work.'

'You will be tomorrow. I shall arrange it for you with Miss Grant. Tomorrow we will go out and enjoy ourselves.'

'Okay,' she said, happily. 'Agreed.'

He smiled at her and she felt suddenly

wildly happy.

'See you at dinner,' he said, lightly.

*   *   *

Hilary was feeling off-colour again when Dorna found her in her room.

'It's that beer I drank at the tombs,' she complained. 'It has upset me. What did you get from the "antiques" village?'

'Heaps,' said Dorna so happily that the old woman looked at her suspiciously, then she relaxed as Dorna began to show her the carved pieces she had bought, and the drawing she had done. The girl certainly knew and loved her work.

'These are good,' she acknowledged, 'very good, in fact. Do you plan to do more work on them now?'

'No, I've had enough for one day,' said Dorna. 'It's been so very hot.'

'I know. That's troubling me, Dorna. I'm getting older. I can't stand up to it the same, and I've got to be more careful what I eat and drink.'

'I don't think that we have any problem at this hotel ... nor the last one, for that matter,' said Dorna. 'I can't say I would care for Egyptian food, but at these good hotels they do cater to our western tastes.'

'You're right, of course, but don't even mention food at the moment, girl. I told you

120

I'm feeling off-colour and I think the beer disagreed with me. I shall have something sent to my room. Can you arrange your own meals?'

A flush of excitement stained Dorna's cheeks, so that Hilary Grant looked at her more closely.

'You've met someone else you fancy!' she accused. 'I can see it in your face. You young girls are all alike. First it was Simon Elliott, and now some other man. One of these times it will be an Egyptian!'

'Oh, Hilary!'

Suddenly Dorna was laughing and she was about to tell Hilary the truth when she paused a little. There was no reason why she should keep it quiet that Simon had followed her here, but he had asked her to say nothing until he had seen Miss Grant. Perhaps it was best to respect his wishes. And Hilary was unpredictable.

'I am going to my own room,' she said. 'I'm sorry to have disturbed you. I'll go down to dinner and if there's anything I can do for you, let me know.'

'You're a good child, Dorna,' the older woman said, suddenly.

She looked tired and for a moment Dorna's heart misgave her. How old was Hilary Grant? She had to admit to herself that she had no idea. Perhaps all this travelling was upsetting for her.

'Don't forget to let me know if I am needed,' she repeated, then went to her own room.

CHAPTER TEN

In her room Dorna rested for as long as she dared, then she showered, washing the dust of the day out of her lovely honey-gold hair. She found a rustling apricot silk dress with pretty frills edged with gold embroidery at the neck and wrists, and a pair of matching gold sandals; then she touched her golden skin lightly with make-up and put a tiny dab of her most expensive perfume onto her handkerchief.

Dorna had always cared more about her work than her looks, but now a critical look in the mirror assured her that she was looking her best.

In the diningroom she found Simon waiting for her, and his eyes lit up with gold lights when she walked forward.

'My, my,' he said, admiringly, 'I don't know if I've mentioned it, but you are a very beautiful woman, Miss Dorning. I'm glad I've staked a claim on you tonight, or someone might have been cutting me out.'

She coloured prettily and laughed.

'You don't look too bad yourself, Mr Elliott.'

'What about Miss Grant? Have you told her?'

'You said not to.'

'That's right I did, but she has eyes. I had expected you both to appear, and I was about to explain my presence here.'

'She's not coming down. Her tummy is upset again.'

'Oh.' The mischief faded from Simon's golden eyes. 'Oh, I am sorry to hear that. You might have guessed that Miss Grant has not been one of my most favourite people, but I don't wish her ill, especially with that sort of upset.'

'Why were you so much against her?' she asked. 'Can't you tell me?'

'I *have* told you. I've no bad feeling towards her at all this evening,' he said, his smile returning. 'Are we having dinner alone? I can't think of anything nicer. Let's order a superb meal and some wine. Let's forget everything else, and enjoy ourselves.'

It was an evening of enchantment for Dorna. She ate prawn cocktail and as much delicious salad and fruit as she wanted. The light wine which Simon chose was delicious, and after dinner there was a floor show, the highlight being a wonderful performance by a well-known belly dancer who swayed almost hypnotically to strange sweet music. Dorna felt languorous and deeply happy as, later, she danced in Simon's arms. But soon the warmth and excitement of the day, followed by a wonderful evening, took their toll and she felt very tired.

'I shall see you to your room,' Simon said, quietly, and she nodded and picked up her wrap and purse. He opened the door of her bedroom, then followed her inside and as she turned to him, suddenly she was in his arms and all else was forgotten as her body seemed to turn to fire whilst his hands held her lightly and possessively.

Never before had she allowed a man to touch her like this, but as his lips claimed hers again, she knew that Simon meant more to her than anyone she had ever known before. Whatever happened, she loved him desperately.

'Darling Dorna,' he whispered, 'do you really want me to stay? I could never do anything to hurt you, or upset you.'

'I want you to stay,' she whispered, and a moment later she undid the straps of her beautiful gown, and allowed it to slip to the floor.

Simon removed his jacket and they gazed at one another then, as he made a move towards her, the telephone suddenly jangled and Dorna's heart leapt with fright. The noise was like a great jangling alarm bell intruding into her consciousness.

With trembling fingers she picked it up and listened to Hilary's rather harsh voice.

'I wondered when you were going to get

back to your room. Can you come in and see me, Dorna?'

'I'm undressing, ready for bed,' she said, almost without thinking.

'I shan't keep you, but I feel off-colour. My sight is poor in artificial light and I want to take a tablet which should put me right. Can you come in and help me?'

'Certainly I will,' said Dorna, rather wearily.

She felt almost sick as she put down the telephone and for a moment she could hardly bear to turn to Simon. What *would* he think of her? She had been about to offer all of herself to him. He must think her very fair game. She could not explain to him that she had done it because she could not help herself, because the love she felt for him was so great that she wanted only him.

Shameful colour stained her cheeks and her head dropped forward so that her silky golden hair lay like a curtain against her cheeks.

'I ... I'm sorry,' she said, huskily.

Simon had come to sit beside her, and now he tried to pull her into his arms, but this time she resisted.

'I shouldn't have asked you to stay.'

She could hardly meet his eyes and after a careful scrutiny, he turned her face towards him.

'Look at me, Dorna.'

She opened her eyes and stared at him, but the hunger for him was no longer on her face.

The shame was still there.

'*I* asked to stay. You did not ask me. I asked because I wanted you desperately, my dear. I still do.'

'I ... I've got to go. Miss Grant isn't feeling well. She needs a tablet, and her eyesight is poor at night. I must go and help her.'

He put his hands on either side of her cheeks, then bent to kiss her lightly on the lips.

'Get up early in the morning,' he said, 'unless Miss Grant is really ill. If she is going to be okay, advise her to have a quiet day and we will spend the day sightseeing. We will forget this evening. Will that make you happy?'

She did not answer. The reaction to all that had gone before left her feeling dead inside, but Simon was shaking her gently.

'Tomorrow, Dorna darling? Here's my room number, if you need me.'

He had put on his jacket and was wrapping her up in her long housecoat.

'Go and see to Hilary Grant, then get a good sleep. Don't worry about anything. Call me if you need me.'

That's what she had told Hilary, thought Dorna. Now Hilary did need her.

'Okay, tomorrow morning,' she agreed.

'Goodnight, Dorna.'

Again he bent and kissed her, then he was gone. She fastened the belt of her housecoat and went to see Hilary.

*　　*　　*

Hilary Grant was almost asleep when Dorna went into her room, but she roused herself when the girl found her tablets and gave her one on her tongue, with a sip of bottled water.

'You were talking to a man,' she accused. 'I heard you. You had taken a man to your room.'

Dorna flushed. 'Surely it's not a crime to talk to a man.'

'You said you were getting ready to go to bed.'

Dorna's cheeks deepened in colour. 'You can't make judgments over what I intended. You were not there to see and, in any case, I must be free to make my own friends as I wish. As a matter of fact, he and I are going sightseeing tomorrow.'

'Oh?'

Suddenly Hilary was wide-awake.

'You intend to go sight-seeing with this man?'

Dorna nodded. 'You agreed that I should have time off when I want it. I think I'd better tell you now that the man is Simon Elliott. He has moved on here from Cairo. We met today after I left you.'

Hilary's brows drew together and she tightened her lips.

'He was following us! I should have known he would do that. How stupid! Yet it's easy to see what is in his mind. Oh well, I can't stop you going with him except to warn you not to get involved.'

Dorna had been expecting a display of anger, but instead Hilary only looked tired as she leaned back on her pillows.

'I can't stop you,' she repeated, 'by telling you I need you for work. I will need to rest here for a couple of days. I know how much my old bones can take these days and I shall not be able to work tomorrow nor, I would think, the day after. You are quite free. Where do you plan to go with Mr Elliott?'

'Aswan.'

'Aswan. Abu Simbel also, I expect. As a matter of fact, I had planned to make that part of our itinerary, but . . . but it is very frustrating that I am not up to it. My digestion troubles me badly and my heart is not strong enough to stand up to a vigorous programme. If you must know, that's one reason why I wanted a healthy young girl like you to take on part of the work load. I would be grateful if you would do a little work while you are there.'

Hilary's tone had become so very mild after the hectorings Dorna had received that the girl's concern began to mount.

'I don't think I *can* go and leave you like this.'

'Like what?' The whiplash was back and the black eyes stared at her balefully.

'You are tired and . . . and it seems to me that

you have been weakened,' said Dorna, anxiously.

Hilary stared back at her.

'I told you, I will rest for two or three days, then I wish to go back to the Museum at Cairo, after which we will fly home. You said you did not want to be away from London for too long in any case, did you not? I hope you will have seen enough of Mr Elliott by then. By the way, I would imagine you will require to stay overnight at Aswan. I hope you understand that.' The hooded eyes looked speculative. 'I shall leave you to make your own arrangements since you are so independent.'

Dorna looked at her uneasily. She would have felt happier if Hilary Grant had lost her temper and told her she must not go anywhere with Simon. That would have been more in character. But this calm acceptance, even encouragement, was disconcerting, including the remarks that she would be expected to remain in Aswan overnight.

'Why did you suddenly decide to avoid Simon Elliott?' she asked.

'Oh, I'm no longer desirous of avoiding him, especially now he has found you again. I do not want my work interrupted by the possibility of unpleasantness, but I should have known he would follow us here. He is your watchdog, Dorna, but I am warning you not to get yourself too involved with him. He will no doubt soon lose interest in you when he satisfies himself that I shall not do you any harm.'

Dorna was frowning. 'I don't understand,' she said, puzzled.

'His wife, my dear. He identifies you with his wife. And he holds me responsible . . . in part, if he is honest . . . for her death.'

'Responsible for his wife's death!'

'Yes. It's very clear to me that that is how he feels. She was a poor-spirited little thing and fancied herself a photographer.'

'Simon said she was very good.'

'Perhaps, in some things. She was a very pretty young woman and rather full of herself, and I was asked by my agents to consider her work for the book I was doing at the time. I took her with me to Greece, but from the start she made things difficult. She wanted to take pictures from all angles such as would have been suitable for some newspapers, but quite wrong for my book. I tried to explain to her that we were not there to photograph some sort of crisis. I only wanted a good craftsman, or craftswoman, in this case. We quarrelled, and finally she took herself off in high dudgeon, leaving me to finish as best I could. Later we had to discard most of her work. It would not have been necessary if only she had listened to my point of view and had not been so determined to get *her* own way.'

Dorna sat down beside Hilary on the bed.

'What happened later?' she asked.

'That was it as far as I was concerned, but I understood that Gillian Vass ... that was her professional name ... had tried to obtain another commission, but in my anger I had complained about her unsatisfactory work to a publisher friend of mine and this complaint was indirectly responsible for Gillian being denied the commission. I heard later that she had also lost other work. She had become very emotional and hysterical about it, and later, also, I learned from my agent that she blamed me. She thought I was using my money and influence to block her career and she had become very depressed and took an overdose of sleeping tablets.'

'How ... how awful,' said Dorna.

Hilary Grant leaned back tiredly.

'I only heard most of this tale after this sad event, and when I heard of her death I was naturally upset and sent flowers of condolence. I attended the funeral, and saw Mr Elliott there, but only briefly as you can understand. It was only afterwards that I learned he was the husband, and he blamed me for her death. She never talked about her home life when she was with me. All she could think about was her photography. Now I have no doubt that Simon Elliott thinks I make a hobby out of employing young girls to illustrate my books, then ruin their careers if we have a few cross words.'

'But ... but that is just silly!' cried Dorna.

'How could he think such a thing? Surely it only happened once and ... surely you didn't deliberately ruin her career?'

Hilary smiled sadly. 'He was in love with her, Dorna. They had not been married very long, and she was a very beautiful young girl. He has never married since. Perhaps that is not surprising. He is mixing with some of the most beautiful, most glamorous and most intelligent women one could meet. Just consider this Sylvia Parrish. She is on research for him at the moment, but soon she will be doing other things on television, I'm quite sure. No doubt her face will be known to millions one day. He is mixing with women like that, yet he goes to a lot of trouble to keep you in sight, Dorna. Why? Because hate is as strong as love, and I think he hates me. If he blames me for his wife's death, then he is sure to hate me. I think he now believes it is his mission in life to protect any girl who might become involved with me in the same way as his wife. If I had not employed Alex Mann for my last book, I would no doubt have come up against Simon Elliott again before now.'

Dorna's head had fallen forward on her chest. It all made a strange sort of sense, except that it did not explain a great many things. How had Simon Elliott known that Hilary was coming to Egypt, and that she was going along as an illustrator? How had he known that? On the other hand, he had often asked her about how well she was working with Hilary. He had been concerned about that.

But it was not merely concern for *her*, went her thoughts. He would have been equally concerned for *any* girl illustrator. She had thought he was attracted to her, as a person, but instead he had only been concerned for Hilary Grant's young colleague!

And he had wanted to make love to her ... and she had invited him to stay!

Warm colour rushed to her cheeks and she felt deeply humiliated.

'I shall not go to Aswan with Mr Elliott,' she said, quietly, as she rose to her feet.

'No I want you to go,' said Hilary, 'but I thought I would tell you everything so that you are under no illusions about Mr Elliott. But you have more strength of character in your little finger than his wife had in her whole body. You would never be so devastated by one or two setbacks that you would take an overdose, would you? I suppose I should have realized straight away that she was far too unstable for the work I wanted. I can't see you being afraid of losing any of your markets.'

But she *would* be upset if that happened, thought Dorna. After all, she only had herself to depend on, and to pay the bills. But there again, Gillian Vass had had Simon to live for. How could she have forgotten that!

'Telephone me from Aswan and meantime I'll arrange for us to return home from Cairo in

... say ... three days from now. Will that be satisfactory?'

'Perfectly,' said Dorna, quietly.

Slowly she went back to her room. Now this new wonderful feeling of excitement and anticipation which had entered her life seemed to have vanished, leaving her feeling dull and empty. Hilary Grant had torn it to shreds, but she could not blame Hilary this time. In fact, she should be grateful to her. She had shown Dorna the true state of affairs between herself and Simon Elliott.

She had begun to give him the most important place in her life ... the one on whom she was showering the whole of her love. She had thought she meant a great deal to him, also, otherwise why would he bother to seek her out like this, and change his plans so that he could be with her? She had imagined that it meant something. She had thought he must be falling in love with her, too otherwise he could not want to be with her as he did.

Yet Hilary was right. Simon Elliott was a man who was sure to attract many women. He could have any woman he wanted. And he had sought her out because of hate, not because of love. He hated Hilary Grant, and wanted to see that she did not exploit another girl in the way he imagined Hilary had exploited his wife. It did not matter whether Hilary was right, or wrong. It did not alter the facts for Dorna.

But what should she do now? she wondered.

Her instincts were to pack her bags and return home immediately. Yet what awaited her in London? Her cousin would still be at the flat. The flat! She had been going to marry Mark Hazlitt, and how very long ago that seemed! And Mark had not found her attractive enough either. He had soon left her for another girl.

Dorna lay down in misery, then from somewhere deep pride began to stir. As far as Simon Elliott was concerned, nothing was changed. She would find it difficult to call off their sight-seeing trip without an explanation which might reveal her feelings. Yet how could she go with those feelings torn and aching inside her heart. How could she spend a day, or even two days, in his company, feeling as she did?

She would have to take her work with her, and remind herself that her *work* was the most important thing in her life. She would show him that she had not been too impressed by the way he had stormed into her life.

CHAPTER ELEVEN

Dorna slept at last, then woke to the jangling of the telephone, and Simon's deep cheerful voice in her ear.

'Come on, sleepy head, time to get up. I'm

waiting for you in the breakfast room. I'll hire a car for us and I shall see you down here in ten minutes flat.'

'I'd rather go by bus,' she said, swiftly, and heard a small sigh of resignation.

'You'd rather go by bus? As you like. I didn't know you were so partial to bus travel.'

She wasn't, but she was partial to being surrounded by other people, and not to being left alone with Simon. As yet she hardly knew what to say to him. She must try to make the day as ordinary as possible.

Breakfast was a hurried affair of rolls and coffee. Simon's eyes lit up appreciatively when Dorna appeared in a cool pinefrost blue linen suit, trimmed with white daisies, and a pair of comfortable white sandals on her feet. But he frowned a little when he saw that she was carrying the satchel she used for work.

'I thought we were having time off today for sightseeing.'

'Sorry, not this trip. I want to get more drawings and photographs, if necessary.'

'So Hilary Grant did not waste her time last night! Will she appear at any moment and join the party? Are you both on-duty after all?'

Simon looked at her with keen disappointment.

'No, she's resting, but she already has most of the material she might want from today's outing. I haven't got anything, so I shall have to work, I'm afraid. Sorry about that.'

'You don't sound very sorry,' he said, peering at her closely. 'You are a changeable girl, Dorna. Nights bring out the woman in you, but by morning you are once again the dedicated artist, all efficiency for getting on with the job. Can't you relax at all? Ah well, never mind. I shall be happy with the crumbs. At least I can admire you while you work, and no doubt you will recognize my existence when you put your pad and pencil back in your satchel.'

He was smiling and teasing her, the golden lights flickering in his eyes, but she refused to be drawn. She dared not allow him to get any bigger hold on her heart or she was going to be very hurt indeed.

'I think we'd better go,' she said, briskly, 'or that bus will leave without us.'

They drove down the east side of Luxor and in spite of all her resolutions, Dorna began to relax as she sat beside Simon. What woman would not feel a lightness of spirit on such a morning? she wondered, as she looked out at the Nile with all the small boats with one sail, the feluccas, and the dhows, with two. Again she was fascinated by rural Egypt as she watched the women, dressed as usual in black and with water jugs on their shoulders or their heads, swinging casually along the road towards the village.

'Surely they must get tired of wearing black all the time,' she murmured.

'Not all the time,' said Simon. 'Inside their homes they wear brightly-coloured gowns, but their husbands prefer that they do not look attractive to other men ... outside the home, that is. Hence the black garments and covered faces. Maybe it's not such a bad idea, Dorna. I've seen a few admiring glances being cast in your direction.'

'Please don't!' she said, sharply.

'Oh dear, we *are* in a mood!' he said, softly. 'Something has disagreed with you, I think.'

She bit her lip. 'I don't want to sound disagreeable, but it's just that ... well ... we'll all be going home soon, and living our own lives. We will probably never see one another again.'

'Would that worry you?'

'I didn't say that. I mean, I think we ought to treat one another as ... well ... acquaintances.'

'Acquaintances,' he repeated, solemnly.

Gently he took her hand and began to stroke her fingers so that a great electric shock seemed to shoot through her veins, leaving her weak and trembling. He only had to touch her, she thought crossly, and she felt as though her bones were turning to water.

'I have work to do,' she said, huskily. 'I really have. Please try to understand.'

'Okay, I'll do my best to remember. Do I remain a silent shadow behind you all day?'

His words and tone made the situation seem ridiculous and suddenly she was laughing. All right, so one more day was not going to make much difference. Whatever his motives were for seeking her out, the damage was done now in any case. She was in love with him. She could not help herself.

'Of course not,' she said, more gently. 'I'm sorry. I just want to see everything I can, and finish the job I came to do.'

She was looking out at the crudely-built carts which were coming towards them on the road, some pulled by donkeys, others by oxen. Some men were riding donkeys and looked ridiculous as their legs almost touched the ground.

'That is the kind of thing I find so interesting,' she said. 'It is such a marvellous scene.'

Simon relaxed beside her.

'I know how you feel. I often feel anti-social if I want to do some writing. Go ahead, my dear. Draw what you want, and photograph the rest and if you get grumpy, I shall stand it. But I warn you, if you get too grumpy, I might put you over my knee later on. We will have to stop and relax some time, you know, and when that happens I intend to be right there beside you.'

The bus had stopped outside a camel market and Dorna's eyes began to shine. This was just the sort of scene she wanted.

'A good place for me, too,' Simon was grinning. 'What a pity I don't have a hundred camels. If so, I could purchase myself a wife!'

'I'm sure you'll rustle up a hundred from somewhere,' she retorted.

'They are brought here by the Bedouins,' said Simon.

'And who brings along the wives?' asked Dorna. 'Do they do all the bargaining at the camel market? Can we leave the bus here? People are getting out.'

'Certainly, for a short while. Mind all those snake charmers at the door of the bus.'

But his warning came too late. Dorna had swung ahead of him, and at the door of the bus, she suddenly gasped and turned back to cling to Simon's arm. A snake charmer had produced a cobra which seemed to be dancing up in front of her eyes.

'Steady!' said Simon in her ear.

Other snake charmers squatted on the ground whilst their snakes slithered about in the dust, and Dorna clung wildly to Simon's fingers.

'I hate snakes!' she said.

'Don't worry, darling, I'm here,' he said and there was a wealth of comfort in his voice. Nor did he try to take advantage of her sudden fears. He merely held her firmly and comfortingly.

'I would be the same with a thunderstorm,' she said, shakily.

But soon she was sketching the scene at the camel market where camels stood everywhere with one leg tethered so that they could not get away. Dorna sketched in the background scene of the many tents, then recoiled once more when a snake charmer presented his snake, together with a scorpion, for her to admire.

'I think I would like to go back to the bus,' she told Simon, weakly, and he grinned.

'Cheer up. We'll soon reach Edfu and there are lovely flowers and trees at "El Karb".'

'You've done all this before,' she said, almost accusingly.

'Well ... yes, some of it.'

'But I thought we were supposed to be sightseeing together. You talked as though we were going to explore new territory. Now let's understand one another, Simon. I don't want, or need, a watchdog.'

His eyes narrowed. 'Is that why you think I'm here?'

'Aren't you?'

'In a way. Not entirely, though ...'

'I can take care of myself.'

'Even with snakes about?'

She bit her lip. How silly and stupid she could be at times!

'I just hate snakes, that's all. Those snake charmers took me by surprise.'

He took her arm. 'What has Hilary Grant been telling you, Dorna? There is a difference in you ever since you saw her last night. I can feel it.'

'What is there to tell? What do you feel

about *her*, Simon? Do you blame her for . . . for anything?'

She could not remind him about his wife's death. She could not bear to see the hurt in his eyes, if she reminded him.

'We must have a talk, Dorna. Not here. Tonight we will have dinner together, then I think we must learn to understand one another.'

She nodded. They were certainly out of step with one another at the moment.

After leaving Edfu, the home of the Temple of the Falcon God, they drove through a Nubian village which had been built by the government for the people who had been forced to leave their homes when the Aswan Dam was built, and here Dorna worked swiftly and carefully.

'This is marvellous,' she said, 'and just what Hilary wants . . . the very new as well as the ancient. I hope she has plenty of notes on this.'

It was very neat and clean, though sun-baked and completely without trees.

'I suppose you realize that, having opted for the bus, we will have to book in somewhere for the night at Aswan,' said Simon, conversationally.

She had been so busy with her pencil that she scarcely assimilated his remark for a moment but, when she did, she turned to face him.

'Surely that's not necessary. Surely we can get a car back from Aswan.'

He shook his head, his eyes dancing with light.

'Not advisable. It gets very dark suddenly here. In any case, I don't think you should come all the way to Egypt without seeing Abu Simbel, and the great statues of Rameses II, which had to be moved to make way for the dam. It must surely be a highlight of Hilary Grant's book.'

'She has already done work on that.'

'And therefore sees no reason why she should waste time in order to let Dorna look at the place for pleasure. Don't you know that *that* is what I wanted for you today? Just a little bit of pleasure, even if you had to return again later for work with Hilary.'

'I am here for pleasure as well as work. The two are as one to me. And Hilary knows where I am today, and she doesn't mind at all if I relax a little as well as doing what work I can. She is not a slave-driver really.'

He took her arm as they left the bus.

'Now she's beginning to show good sense. We'll book in at the New Cataract Hotel, unless you're a movie buff and watched *Death on the Nile*. It featured the "Old Cataract" hotel across the road.'

'The New Cataract will be fine.'

He slid his hand down her arm, then held her hand.

'One room, Dorna?'

She stiffened. 'Certainly not, Simon. Two

143

rooms, and no hankie-pankie. And I pay all my own expenses.'

He smiled, but his eyes narrowed again.

'Two rooms it is.' Then his teeth flashed in a grin. 'You can always change your mind later.'

She felt the warm colour in her cheeks.

'Look, Simon, I know what you must be thinking. I was quite a pushover the other night. I think it must have been the wine at dinner, or something, but you might as well know that I don't sleep around. I don't condemn other people who want to live that way, but it won't do for me.'

He was looking at her with deep absorption.

'Okay, Dorna. No need to spell it out. I think I told you once before that I would never force you to do what you don't want to do.'

Oh, wouldn't you? she thought, keeping her wits about her. No, he would not force her, but he could so easily break down her defences, and the result would be the same. Simon would never need to force anyone.

Dorna hoped for a room which faced the Nile, but they had booked in late and they were each forced to accept a room at the back of the hotel, the outlook being a village. But again Dorna was fascinated by the life in the village. The houses were made of mud brick, some painted white, and most of them with an outside courtyard with steps going up to the roofs of the houses. Some of the roofs were dirty, but others were neat and clean, and there

144

were a few scattered palm trees.

Dorna had packed a cool, simple dress in lemon silk and she changed into this after a quick wash. Downstairs the hotel staff in light brown uniforms, with baggy trousers fastened at the ankles, full-sleeved shirts braided and buttoned down the front, and each one wearing a red fez, seemed to dash about all over the hotel. Dorna was so fascinated by their appearance that she failed to notice Simon for a moment.

'So you came prepared,' he said, grinning. 'Unfortunately I did not. I need a toothbrush. There is time for us to go to the local bazaar before dinner. How about coming with me?'

'Why not? Do we take a cab?'

'We can do that, of course, or if you like we can walk.'

'We'll walk,' she decided.

There was a long driveway from the hotel to the road and Dorna was fascinated by the beautiful flowers on either side of the drive, and suddenly she was wildly happy again as she took Simon's hand and they hurried out into the main road and the great conglomeration of traffic in which the pedestrian came last. She clung to Simon as he helped her negotiate the honking cabs, horse-drawn carriages, the people in native dress and the many holes in the pavement.

The shops were fascinating and Dorna scarcely noticed how quickly the darkness had set in as she looked at the wicker-work, jewellery, carvings and spices in small bowls. Simon negotiated the purchase of a bead bracelet, then frowned a little when she was about to protest at the gift. He fastened it on to her wrist, then gripped her arm and his eyes told her he would be hurt if she did not accept it.

'Only a small gift in memory of a lovely day,' he said, and she acknowledged it with pleasure.

'I love it, Simon. Thank you.'

'Don't I get a kiss?'

She hesitated, then reached up to kiss his cheek as he pulled her into the shadows, then once again she felt the warm pressure of his lips on her own, and her body felt weak and trembling.

'I wish you would not do that,' she said, huskily.

'Why not? You are a very beautiful girl, Dorna. Is it too much to ask that I won't try to kiss you? And you knew very well that we would have to stay the night here. You brought that pretty dress with you.'

'Hilary said it was possible, unless I got a cab.'

'What would be the sense of that? We haven't seen anything yet.'

She was blushing. 'I think we'd better get back.'

Suddenly the light had gone and everything was strange to her. As they passed a large building on the corner, the curtains had not been drawn and she could see men and young boys at prayer. She was suddenly conscious of the strangeness and mystery of this fascinating country.

'Back to the hotel then,' said Simon, and took her hand again.

At dinner Dorna preferred to drink boiled water instead of wine and Simon grinned, then his eyes grew serious.

'No need to be afraid of me,' he said, quietly. 'I shall not disturb you, Dorna. You've made it very clear how you feel about that, though you can't blame me for trying. But I will only come to you when you want me.'

He had said that he wanted to talk to her, no doubt to tell her about Gillian, but now he was in a silent mood and she could not remind him about it.

But that night, when he said goodnight to her, he merely kissed her cheek and walked to his own room. She had a crazy, almost overwhelming desire to call him back, and only her pride prevented her from doing so.

But she had never felt more restless or dissatisfied with herself as she tried to sleep that night.

CHAPTER TWELVE

The weather was once again very hot as they flew out to see the temple of Rameses II and his Queen Nefertari, statues so huge that she could only gasp with wonder and marvel at the tremendous work which had gone into taking them apart and reassembling them on this new site when the Aswan Dam was built.

'The whole site looks exactly like the original,' Simon told her. 'It's marvellous.'

They mounted the steps of the temple, through the statues and an 'H' shaped doorway. Inside it was cooler, but very stuffy and Dorna examined the two small chapels, the 'birth house' of the sun as it rose each day, and the special room where Rameses sits with his gods and where the sun lights the room and shines on Rameses twice per year.

'That now happens one day from the original schedule,' said Simon, 'owing to the moving of the site.'

'Were they special days?' asked Dorna.

'His coronation day and his birthday, I understand. Do you wish to go into the Temple of Love?' he asked, his golden eyes resting on her face. 'It's a smaller temple of Queen Nefertari.'

'Why not?' asked, Dorna, her eyes challenging his. 'In fact, I think it is quite lovely.'

Later Dorna decided she did not want to see anything else.

'I think Hilary has all she wants on the Aswan Dam, and I've got enough now for my job,' she said to Simon. 'Anything else would be an anti-climax.'

'Well, thank goodness for that,' he grinned. 'Now, perhaps, we can start to enjoy ourselves properly. Let's go back to our hotel for a meal, then we can go up the Nile in a felucca.' His eyes danced into her own. 'Very romantic.'

He had pulled her into the shadows and once again she felt his arms round her and his lips claimed her own. She held out against him for a moment, then she relaxed in his arms. Whatever the future held in store, this was one more moment to savour.

'Dorna, do we have to go back so soon?' he whispered. 'Couldn't we have one day to ourselves? You are so beautiful that I don't want to part with you.'

Once again the languor of temptation swept over her. How easy it would be to say yes. But afterwards? Afterwards when she only had her memories, would she be able to shrug it off and carry on with her work? She had known girls whose careers suffered badly after they had given up everything for some man, then had been unable to pick up the pieces. And she needed to be independent. She needed to earn her living. Mark Hazlitt had backed out of their marriage, and she could not imagine that Simon would ever want to marry her. It would not be sensible to stay here with him.

'Decide after we have eaten,' he said, 'then we'll take one of those blue and white feluccas up the Nile. That should touch your heart even if nothing else does.'

He was smiling at her again, and the warmth of his arm on her shoulders made her want to stay close to him for ever. He had picked up her satchel in which she carried all her drawing equipment, and almost automatically she reached out to take it from him. It was very precious to her. She felt lost without having her notebook handy.

'I'll take it,' she said. 'I don't like to be without it.'

She saw his smile fading a little.

'Another dedicated career woman.'

'That's right. Don't you approve?'

'Sometimes it can be overdone, Dorna.'

'In other words, you would like your woman to put you first.'

A great deal of warmth had gone out of his eyes.

'Perhaps I should,' he agreed. 'I would most certainly expect my woman to put me first.'

Her eyes began to glint. Where would she have been today if she had not had her career? Yet ... if he loved her ... if he loved her as she could so easily love him, wouldn't she do just that? He was the only man for whom she would be sorely tempted to give up everything, but if he truly loved her, wouldn't he take an interest in everything she did, including her career?

Dorna turned away. They had not known one another long enough for that, and she must hide this growing passion for him. She did not want her pride to be trampled in the dust a second time. It must be good for Simon's ego that women found him so attractive that they fell into his arms so easily. Hilary Grant was trying to save her from this sort of humiliation. She must have seen how attracted she was to Simon.

On the other hand, Simon imagined that Hilary had ruined his wife's career and she had been driven into taking extra pills, which had killed her. Was that why Simon now wanted a woman who would put him first?

She did not blame him, thought Dorna, rather sadly. It must have been a great tragedy in his life. Would he ever trust another woman enough for marriage? As far as she was concerned, she wanted the solid ties of marriage in her life ... or nothing.

*　　　*　　　*

After they had eaten at the hotel, Simon escorted Dorna over the road to the courtyard of the Old Cataract Hotel where they descended a series of steps to the landing where the feluccas waited to take them up the Nile.

Dorna's eyes gleamed as she looked at the young man who operated the felucca. Against the blue and white of his boat, with the white sail, he looked a colourful figure in his brown robe with an orange hat consisting of a round top and a wide band. He gripped the robe between his teeth as he leapt off the felucca, in order to tie it up.

He rowed, sitting on a board which was higher than the seats on either side, until they reached the centre of the river where the wind took over, the sails filled out, and Dorna's eyes sparkled with pleasure as they skimmed over the water.

'Now I know a little more about you,' said Simon. 'You like sailing.'

'I love this,' she agreed. 'Oh Simon, I'm so glad I've been able to come on to Aswan with you. It's been wonderful.'

'It would have been a pity to miss it all merely because Miss Grant could not make the trip,' he said, drily.

'Just look at those small boys,' she said with delight, pointing to where a number of youngsters were sailing in the river in tiny boats made of tin cans. Others had nothing more than a board in their hands. A few minutes later the tiny boats were beside the felucca and the children, their huge brown eyes pleading soulfully, were holding out hands for alms.

'They   deserve   something   for   their

enterprise,' Simon laughed, then, as they passed a small rocky island, Dorna's eyes fell on a woman, all in black, doing her washing in the river. Immediately she covered her face with a black veil, though her children ran in the nude up and down the island with complete freedom and abandon. How would she feel if she had to live a restricted life like the woman in black? Dorna wondered.

They sailed up the river to the Aga Khan's tomb, a huge square structure with a dome top, standing high on the sandy hills overlooking the river and the villages to the city beyond.

Simon pointed out a low, very long house, built with the eastern types of arches and verandahs.

'That house belongs to the Begum,' he told her. 'I believe it is called "The House of Love". She goes up the hill each day when she is in residence, to lay a rose on her husband's tomb.'

'Charming idea,' Dorna murmured, and Simon took hold of her hand.

'Would you do the same for me, Dorna?'

'Don't joke,' she said, crossly. 'In fact, I think I've had enough of tombs now to last me a lifetime. It has been wonderful, but . . .'

'But tomorrow we'll roam round the bazaars and see what we can find,' Simon suggested.

'I don't know about tomorrow.'

'Just one more day, Dorna.'

The golden lights were back in his eyes and his slender but strong fingers held her own lightly. She was very much aware of him. Could she? Which was the stronger, her desire for him, or her commonsense? She had argued each point in her head until she was tired. *Should* she stay for another day? Was it wrong to want even more precious memories to take back with her? Was it sensible? She did not know what the future might hold, but it was very tempting to live for today and to share Simon with no one else for that day. She might even regret it for the rest of her life if she turned away this chance to be more wildly happy than she had ever been in her life.

'All right,' she whispered, huskily, 'just one more day.'

She saw the flame of desire and delight leaping into his eyes, and he sighed very softly as though he had been holding his breath.

'You won't regret it, Dorna darling,' he said, softly, 'Maybe, then, you will realize that we have something rather precious between us. Maybe, too, we can have that talk I promised you. There is a lot we have to iron out.'

*　　*　　*

They returned to the hotel and Simon walked to the reception desk to make arrangements for one more night at the hotel.

'There is message for you, sir,' one of the men informed him, 'to make telephone call. This is number.'

154

Simon looked taken aback.

'It's the hotel where we stayed in Cairo,' he said to Dorna. 'Wait a moment.'

He crossed to the telephone and Dorna waited, then, turned quickly away as she could hear his voice coming to her clearly.

'Hello? Yes ... Mrs Parrish ... hello, Sylvia? You still there...?'

So it was Sylvia Parrish ... *Mrs* Parrish, she thought, her cheeks flushing a little.

Suddenly she felt as though she had landed badly on solid ground after her feet had been up in the air. She had forgotten about the Sylvia Parrishes in Simon's life. She had been about to add to their numbers.

Simon put down the telephone and hurried over to speak to her.

'Look, darling, I've got to make a longish telephone call. It's work. Something's come up about the current project. Wait for me in the lounge, will you? I'll be with you as soon as possible. I've just got to get some papers from my room.'

He hurried away and she looked round aimlessly. Her joy had begun to evaporate and she felt that she was getting into something she could not handle.

Nearby two American ladies were negotiating the hiring of a car to take them back to Luxor in order to join their tourist group, and suddenly Dorna was galvanized into action. She must get away. She must think

155

about Simon rather more deeply before agreeing to his suggestion.

'Pardon me,' she said to one of the women. 'Please ... would you help me? I would like to reach Luxor also. Would it be possible for me to share your car? I would be most happy to pay whatever is required.'

The women turned to stare at her closely for a few moments, but there was no hesitation on the part of either.

One of them smiled widely. 'Sure you can. Glad to have you along.'

'I'll just get my bag. Won't keep you a moment,' Dorna said and made for the stairs after asking for her bill.

Dorna quickly packed her bag and ran to join the American ladies in the foyer. Simon was still on the telephone and he appeared to be having a long, absorbed conversation. Swiftly she scribbled a note and left it for him at the desk when she paid her bill, though a moment later she saw Simon looking round for her, and managed to avoid him adroitly. She did not want to give him long explanations of her sudden decision, and she certainly did not want to listen to his excuses. He was perfectly entitled to hold long conversations with Sylvia Parrish, and to read Dorna lectures about preferring his women to pay more attention to him than to their own careers. Well, she had a career which demanded a lot of attention. She must be sensible and put that first.

The American ladies were waiting with welcoming smiles beside the hired car, and it was quickly loaded and ready to take off when once again Dorna saw that Simon had come out of the hotel and was looking for her.

Neatly she slipped into the car and they took off at great speed.

'If the driver goes like this all the way, we will be waiting for our group in Jordan,' one of the ladies remarked. 'By the way, I am Amy Lunn and this is my friend, Tina Barry.'

'Jane Dorning,' said Dorna.

She hoped they would not ask her too many questions on the way to Luxor. Now she could hardly believe that this had happened, when only a short time ago she had expected ... she had expected so much, her heart said, and the pain was suddenly so sharp that it left her breathless. She had acted on impulse. Had it been a dreadful mistake?

Shouldn't she have allowed Simon time to explain things? He had said he wanted to talk to her, and to explain his point of view. Was it wrong of her to run away as she had? He would no doubt be so hurt and angry that he would never want to see her again.

Reaction set in and Dorna's heart felt heavy, and there was a harsh lump in her throat which threatened to dissolve in tears.

She leaned back and closed her eyes.

'I guess Miss Dorning is tired,' said Amy Lunn, kindly.

'If her feet are anything like mine, she'll sure be tired,' said Tina. 'I was very sore tempted to duck them into the Nile.'

CHAPTER THIRTEEN

Two days later Dorna, with Hilary Grant beside her, flew home to London.

Hilary's rest at Luxor had given her a new lease of energy and strength, and she had done a considerable amount of work on her book. She had planned to revisit the Museum at Cairo, but when Dorna returned from Aswan Hilary had already decided that she had enough material for the book she wanted to write.

She had cast a shrewd look at Dorna and beyond asking one or two questions about her trip to Aswan and looking at the drawings she had done, she had kept her own counsel with regard to Simon Elliott.

However the following day curiosity got the better of her, especially when Simon did not return to their hotel.

'I thought he was going to see you safely back into my care,' she said, probingly.

Dorna's feelings were raw and sore.

'I don't need anyone to nursemaid me,' she said. 'I enjoyed my trip to Aswan with Mr Elliott and now it is over. I have done quite a lot of work, and I think I've got all we might need. I shall have to do a great deal of work on whichever drawings you want to use, as soon as I get back home, but if we work out a time schedule, I promise to keep to it. I don't think you will be disappointed with the finished work, Hilary.'

'I'm sure I won't child,' Hilary Grant sighed. 'Something tells me that this may be the last book I shall write in this fashion. I'm too old now.'

'Oh no, surely not!'

'Old and tired,' Hilary repeated. 'Well, at least Mr Elliott will be relieved and won't need to check on me another time in case I harass the lives out of young innocent women!'

'Oh, Hilary you exaggerate!' said Dorna. 'I think it is all in the past now.'

'Maybe it is, yet I wonder how he came to be here, following us around, if he were *not* checking up on me. I've mainly had men artists since Gillian, and you're the first young girl since his wife. Would he have dogged my footsteps if I had worked with other young women, I wonder?'

Dorna said nothing. Hilary was rather introspective at times.

'It was a tragedy for the young man, of course, That I will accept. But, you know, he should not blame me. I think he does so in order to forget the real tragedy, that his pretty young wife thought more about her career than she did about him.'

Dorna stared at her. 'How can you know that?'

'It's obvious, child. If she really loved her husband, would it have mattered if no one liked her work, or felt it was unsatisfactory, so that it was returned to her? Wouldn't she have shrugged her shoulders and turned to her young husband for comfort, then showed that she loved him best by putting it all behind her? That's what a young wife deeply in love with her husband would have done.'

Dorna nodded. Of course Hilary was right. Then suddenly she was remembering the intensity of Simon's gaze when he asked her how much her work meant to her. Did it mean everything to her? And he had told her that he expected the woman he loved to put *him* first. She began to understand him a little better, and her heart was greatly touched. If he loved her as he had loved Gillian, of course she would put him first. He must have been very hurt once. Now she might have hurt him again. She should not have left him in such a fashion. She should have waited for him in the hotel, but now it was too late. She would probably never see him again.

'I suppose men can be badly hurt by women, and women by men,' Hilary was saying. 'I was hurt once, Dorna. Oh yes, I wasn't always old and ugly. Once I was young and in love, and planning my own marriage. But I found out he was already married, and that he had never even been estranged from his wife. I was only a ... a diversion, an entertainment, someone to relieve the boredom. I think that's what hurt.'

She was silent, her eyes full of memories.

'I could not see you being used as entertainment value, my dear, but ... but I could so easily have been wrong. I often am these days. If I've spoilt anything for you, I would be very sorry, Dorna.'

'There was nothing to spoil,' said Dorna, tonelessly.

At London Airport they shared a taxi, and as they parted company outside Hilary's home, the older woman kissed the girl's cheek.

'Of course we'll be in touch professionally, but come and see me sometime, my dear. I don't want to lose touch.'

'Of course I will,' Dorna promised.

*　　*　　*

Dorna's cousin, Alison Reid, was still in possession of her flat. She had rung Alison from the airport and the younger girl had promised to have a meal waiting for her when she arrived back at the flat.

'And a hot bath,' said Dorna. 'I feel I will never get rid of the feeling of having sand in my shoes.'

'I know what you mean,' said Alison, rather nervously. 'I'll switch on the immersion heater for you, Dorna. It should be just right when you get here.'

There was evidence of a very hurried tidying-up job when Dorna arrived home, and Alison appeared from the kitchen looking flushed and rather wispy.

'Sorry I haven't done such a good job on the cleaning, but Sheila Agnew has just gone home and she was not the tidiest of people. It was difficult to do anything with her stuff all around, but I'll really work on it tomorrow, Dorna. Cross my heart.'

'That's okay,' said Dorna, rather wearily.

It was not the best of homecomings. She loved her flat but now it looked tatty and uninviting, though she was grateful for Alison's presence. It prevented her from thinking too much. Somehow she would have to forget she had ever met Simon Elliott, but how difficult it was going to be. Over the next few weeks she would be spending her time doing final copies of the sketches and photographs Hilary had chosen and these would be taken along to Liz Paige. Each one of them would hold a memory for her.

'I've made a curry,' said Alison, brightly, 'though here's a cup of tea for now. I'm hot stuff on curries, if you'll excuse the awful pun.'

'Thanks, Alison.'

The curry was very good, but again Alison would not allow her to go into the kitchen, and Dorna knew by the feverish activity that it was far from presentable in its present state.

'Is the water hot?' she asked. 'I would like my bath now, then I think I will go straight to bed.'

'Er ... I think it will be okay now,' said Alison, lamely.

Dorna cleaned the bath, then changed her bed linen.

'I guess I'm learning what a lot of work my mother does,' said Alison, ruefully. 'I used to think a house kept clean by itself.'

Dorna turned to her, then she smiled. Alison looked like a small schoolgirl.

'It's a lesson we all have to learn, dear,' she said. 'We can talk about it tomorrow. Do you mind if we do without that record player for this evening? It is rather loud.'

'Sure. I shan't play it at all.'

She put on the television instead, and Dorna punched her pillow as she listened to an old gangster movie through the wall. Surely they must all be dead by now, she thought until, at last, she was overcome by fatigue.

*   *   *

Alison's presence was truly a mixed blessing thought Dorna as she began, next day, systematically to clean her flat. She was annoyed by the neglect she found, but that irritation kept her from thinking too deeply and she was glad of the physical work.

Alison climbed out of her bed around eleven o'clock and protested that Dorna should have made her get up.

'Who called you when I was not here?' she asked.

'I just sleep very deeply, that's all,' said Alison. 'Have you had breakfast? Shall I make coffee?'

'If you promise to mop up any mess you make.' Then she relented. 'Oh, okay go ahead. Make it for both of us. When are you going home, Alison?'

The younger girl's face flushed.

'Well ... I was hoping you would let me stay a couple more weeks to see if I can land a job in London. It's hopeless up home. Besides, I think I would like it here so much better.'

'I'm sorry, darling, but I don't think I can share with you,' said Dorna, firmly. 'Didn't Aunt Claire say you still have to go back to school? You see, this is my place of work, as well as my home and I have to start to do a great deal of work. I could not put up with your mess, Alison. You would drive me round the bend.'

'Oh, please, Dorna, just for two weeks,' Alison pleaded. 'Then I shall find my own place, I promise, either here or back home. I want to leave school. It isn't doing anything for me. Mummy will let me stay on here if I'm with you, I'm quite sure, and if I get a job and somewhere else that is nice, she won't mind.

164

You can talk her into it for me.'

'Thanks a lot,' said Dorna.

She ruminated for a while. How could she put up with Alison for two whole weeks?

'Oh, by the way, your boyfriend has been ringing quite often. I said you were still in Egypt.'

'Boyfriend? Which boyfriend?' Dorna's heart leapt. Had Simon been trying to get in touch with her?

'He didn't give his name, but he sounded very impatient,' said Alison. 'He sounded a bit peeved because you were not here.'

'Oh.'

'I thought you had broken your engagement,' said Alison. 'I expect you've got a lot of boyfriends, though. I mean, it's easier to meet more boys in London and have more fun. Not like home. It's deadly dull there because you can't bring them home for parties and things...'

'Have you been having parties in my flat?' Dorna demanded.

'No, of course not.' Alison's voice had a false ring to it. 'You said not to. I'm talking about *you*. I'd like to meet lots more boys while I'm here. I'd like to have a good time before I have to go back home.'

Dorna sighed. She was also going to have to think seriously about Alison, but it seemed to her that she would have to be returned home as soon as possible. Aunt Claire would never get over it if anything happened to Alison and she would complain to Dorna's mother. It would be a family row.

As Dorna had suspected, a steady stream of youngsters began to arrive at the flat, and she grew to be expert at getting rid of them.

Her temper was not at its best when she opened the door to yet another ring, and found Mark Hazlitt on the doorstep.

'Oh ... Oh, it's you, Mark,' she said, taken aback. 'I thought it was some young man with pink and green hair calling on Alison again.'

'That's the sultry-voiced female on the telephone,' said Mark. 'She kept informing me that you were in Egypt.'

'So it was you!' said Dorna, and could hardly hide her sick disappointment. Yet how could she expect Simon to get in touch with her now?

'Of course it was me. Who did you think it was? You haven't got someone else, have you, Dorna?'

Mark had followed her in and his eyes were anxious as he looked at her.

'I've been trying so hard to get in touch with you, Dorna darling. I was beginning to think you'd never get home, and I was never going to sort out this mess.'

'What mess?' she asked. 'Sit down, Mark. You look upset. Would you like a drink, or would coffee do? I haven't got much in with having Alison around. She entertains far too many of her young friends and they appear to have eaten everything up like locusts.'

'I don't want anything,' said Mark, 'except to talk to you. I've got to get things sorted out, you see. Dorna! Dorna, darling, I made an awful mistake. I didn't realize how much I loved you, until it was too late. I just couldn't reach you. You had gone.'

'You mean Miss ... what was her name? ... Ardath? ... has turned you down,' she said, gently. 'I'm so sorry, Mark.'

He shook his head.

'I didn't even ask her, darling. If you remember Sir Kenneth Ardath offered me a marvellous job in Scotland and I was invited to a house party for the weekend so that we could discuss it, but ... but somehow it did not feel right. I felt strange with those people, Dorna, and I began to remember all we had hoped and planned to do. I began to remember how happy we had been together, and I found that I didn't want what Sir Kenneth offered. I only wanted everything as it had been. I only wanted you, but when I rang here, you had gone to Egypt. I've done work out there myself and, in fact, I was planning to go there and find you if you had not returned home.'

He waited hopefully for a few minutes.

'That's how much it would have meant to me, to have you back again, darling.'

Mark reached out and pulled her into his arms and began to kiss her passionately, but

Dorna held herself rigid. Unbelievably she found Mark's kisses distasteful. She did not want him to touch her. He stared into her eyes, then let her go, a hurt look on his face.

'You're going to make things difficult, aren't you?' he asked, rather huffily. 'Sometimes I was afraid you would, then I would think you were above that sort of thing. It would not be worthy of you. You were never petty, Dorna. I'll say that for you.'

'No, I don't think I have been petty,' she agreed. She looked at him rather wearily. This past few days had been very exhausting, and now Mark's visit was not helping. How different he appeared to her now. How could she ever have imagined herself in love with Mark Hazlitt? Even his appearance was unattractive, yet she had come very close to marriage with him. She had thought her heart was broken when she found out that his plans were very different from her own.

Now he only appeared to her as a rather petulant young man who always liked his own way, and who was not at all pleased to be turned down.

'We could carry out all our original plans, Dorna,' he was saying, eagerly. 'I mean, I know I made an awful mistake, and I have to ask you to forgive me, darling, but I've learned my lesson, and I promise it will never happen again. I mean it will be all the better now. It's better that I have made a mistake and realized it, then I won't make it again, ever. I know you are worth far more than any other girl and I will never walk out on you again. You see? I promise, Dorna.'

Suddenly the door of the flat opened and Alison bounced in, accompanied by another girl and two young men. They were all giggling noisily. Alison greeted Dorna with a delightful smile and looked curiously at Mark.

'I've brought Julian and Sue home for coffee,' she said happily. 'And Dave has bought a new disc. Are you busy, Dorna, or can we listen to it on the record player? Oh...' she stopped and stared at Mark. 'I've just thought...'

'This is Mark Hazlitt,' said Dorna, briefly. 'My cousin Alison and friends.'

'The voice on the phone,' said Mark.

'Oh yes,' said Alison, blushing when she remembered the sultry tones she had used.

'Can we use the record player, Alison?'

'For God's sake, can't we go down to the café at the end of the road and talk?' asked Mark, turning to her as the record player was turned on.

'Nothing to talk about,' Dorna said above the din. 'I'm sorry, Mark, but you were right first time. It would not have worked. We were not really right for one another.'

'Now you're being vindictive,' said Mark, angrily. Music blared forth into the flat and Mark looked incensed as he stared at her.

'I wanted to talk this thing out. You cannot give me a fair hearing with all this racket.'

'Oh, very well,' she conceded. 'I've got to go out, anyway. We'll talk it out, but you might as well know that my mind is made up, Mark. I'm sorry but that's just the way I feel now.'

They walked to the café, dodging the traffic as they crossed the road while Mark held her arm. Dorna was reminded of the traffic at Aswan when Simon had held her hand before they made a mad dash across the street, arriving laughing and breathless on the other side. How wonderful it had been to share his company. But, of course, she loved Simon.

She had also loved Mark at one time, she reminded herself and now it was all over. He was just another young man and she had no feeling for him other than friendship. Would it be the same with Simon one day? She shook her head at the thought, knowing that her love for Simon was so much greater than her love for Mark had ever been.

'It's no use,' she told him, when he had brought over a tray with two cups of coffee, hot but bitter. 'It's no use, Mark, I don't love you any more. I'm very sorry, but ... but that's how I feel.'

'That's only because I hurt you. Give me another chance, Dorna, and I'll make it up to you,' he pleaded. 'I know I can get you back, if you'll only meet me half-way and allow me to make it up to you. We could have fun

170

together again.'

She was shaking her head. 'No, Mark. I'm sorry.'

'You've met someone else,' he said, accusingly.

She paused, then nodded. 'Yes.'

'Who?'

'No one you know. Anyway, nothing will come of it. I probably shan't ever see him again.'

He looked at her smudged eyes and tried to take her hand.

'I won't stay out of your life while there is no one else,' he said, firmly. 'He must be mad not to snap you up.'

Dorna's lips twisted. She hated to remind Mark but there had been a time when he could have 'snapped her up'.

'I shan't change my mind,' she said, gently. 'It's no use really, Mark.'

'We'll see,' he said. 'This coffee is terrible.'

'I can't spend any more time on it,' said Dorna, looking at her watch. 'I have shopping to do. I'm running out of my supplies.'

'I'll be back,' Mark told her. 'Maybe you'll change your mind when you've thought about it.'

*   *   *

Dorna walked home feeling tired and frustrated. She had lots of work to do, and she

171

seemed to have hands pulling at her in all directions. She did not want to upset Aunt Claire, but enough was enough, and Alison would have to go home. She would no longer be responsible for her young cousin.

When she let herself in with her own key, the music was as brash as ever, but Alison sprang up from sitting on a cushion on the floor and ran towards her with shining eyes.

'Did you see him?' she asked.

'You know very well I have seen him,' said Dorna, crossly. 'Mark and I had to go out to the café at the corner in order that we could talk. We drank some terrible coffee.'

'Not *that* one, the other one,' said Alison. 'Oh, Dorna, he was gorgeous, wasn't he, Sue? Wasn't he, Julian?'

Julian stared at her sulkily, but Sue was enthusiastic in agreeing with Alison.

Dorna's heart began to beat rapidly.

'You mean someone else called to see me? Did he leave a name?'

'No, nothing like that. He just asked if you were here and looked around at us as though he had put us under the microscope. I said you were out at the café with your boyfriend, and he looked a bit grim, then left. But he was tall, with lovely closely-curled hair and one of those tropical island complexions, like he was selling Bounty bars on television. Sue and I just stared. Then he left.'

Dorna's heart seemed to drop into her shoes.

So Simon had been here! How welcoming it must have seemed to him, this pretty flat of which she had been so proud. Now it was again littered with magazines, coats, bags, mugs and paper cartons. And Alison had told him that she was out with her boyfriend! Dorna could have kicked the furniture with frustration.

Later that evening she told Alison that she was going to send her home.

'It's no use, darling,' she said. 'I've got work to do and I am not getting on with it while the flat is so disturbed. I just can't have you here. You can come back in a year or two when you've grown up a little, and had most of your noisy fun.'

'Fat chance at home,' said Alison, sulkily. 'Daddy is always complaining about my record player and "Top of the Pops" and he makes horrible remarks about my favourite pop groups. And Mummy is not much better. She won't allow me to touch my hair, and I would love to do it like Toyah.'

But already Dorna was on the telephone and talking to Aunt Claire.

'I quite understand, darling,' her aunt said, briskly. 'I was going to get in touch with you anyway. Alison has had enough holiday now. Just put her on the train, Jane dear, and we'll look out for her at this end.'

'Thanks, Aunt Claire. I'm sorry about it, but...'

'Oh, thank you for having her, dear. I didn't

think you would put up with her all this time. It's very good of you to spend your time on Alison when I know you have work to do.'

Dorna looked at Alison sternly when she put down the telephone.

'Aunt Claire doesn't know I've been away. You didn't tell her.'

'Neither did you,' said Alison, sulkily. 'She would not have let me come if I had mentioned it.'

'I only let you have the flat on certain conditions. I did ask you and Sheila not to fill the flat with men friends.'

'And I made no promises. Besides we had plenty of girls here, too. And you *did* invite me, Dorna, you know you did.'

'I made a mistake,' said Dorna, 'though I'll also remind you of the number of times you wrote inviting yourself. Okay, so we accept that it's my fault, but now you go home to Aunt Claire.'

'Well, I think you're being mean,' said Alison.

She flounced off to pack her bags.

*   *   *

She seemed to have made a lot of mistakes, thought Dorna, rather grimly, as she settled down to work at last. The flat was now quiet and orderly, but it was a long time before she felt that she was doing good work and much

174

time had been lost.

Dorna answered the telephone so often to Alison's teenage friends that she stopped answering it altogether. She had now grasped hold of her project and the work was coming to life under her skilful fingers. She worked long hours and with deep concentration, but finally she had a finished series of drawings all ready to deliver to Liz Paige.

She rang up for an appointment and went along the following afternoon at three o'clock.

CHAPTER FOURTEEN

'Well! What on earth have you been doing to yourself?' asked Liz, as she greeted Dorna with anxious eyes. 'I expected you to look blooming after your sojourn in Egypt, but here you are with a wee white face and dark circles under your eyes. What happened? Did Hilary Grant give you a bad time?'

'Why do you ask that?' Dorna sat down and shot a keen glance at Liz.

'Oh, she has the reputation, but I was pretty confident that you could handle her. She's getting a television series, you know. I think Simon Elliott has been pulling a few strings.'

'Simon Elliott! Pulling strings for Hilary!'

Dorna was astonished. Hilary must have been wrong about him then, she thought. She had been so convinced that he blamed her for losing his wife, and hated her for it. But instead he was helping to arrange a television series for her and making everything she had dreamed about come true. Hilary must certainly have been wrong about Simon!

Liz's sharp eyes noted the sudden rise in colour in Dorna's cheeks when Simon's name was mentioned, but she said nothing until she started to examine Dorna's work.

'Hilary's work is already in, of course,' she said. 'These look marvellous, Dorna. I'm sure she will be pleased. I understand you went all independent on her and paid all your own expenses after all. I expect your fees for this work will cover it a-plenty. I doubt if she'll have any complaints this time.'

'Does she usually complain?' Dorna asked.

'Frequently, but we soon get it ironed out. Insults get exchanged, but we all know her, and we know she doesn't really mean it.'

'No, I don't think she does,' said Dorna. 'I think she's so busy sorting out her own ideas, that all other remarks are just background music, but I also think she can get a bee in her bonnet at times.'

'Then you enjoyed the trip with her?'

'Very much. It was an ... an experience.'

Liz smiled as she put the drawings carefully into their folder.

'Keep all your sketches, won't you? We might not be finished yet. Others may have to be chosen. So Simon Elliot caught up with you okay.'

The remark caught Dorna by surprise, and once again the colour stained her face.

'You know him, Liz?'

'Very well. Last time he was in the office, just before you went to Egypt, he called to see me and there on the desk was the photograph which we had taken at our last Christmas party. Remember? The one with you sitting next to me. Well, Simon was very taken, and even more so when he knew you were going with Hilary. He said he had a project in hand which would also take him to Cairo, and wanted to know where you would be staying and when. I thought it would do no harm to tell him. He's pure gold all through is Simon, and he is one of the finest men I know. But he did have a thing about Hilary at one time.'

'I know,' said Dorna. 'His wife worked with her, then ... then things went bad for her.'

'Yes, it was a sorry business,' Liz agreed. 'She was such a highly-strung little thing, and she worried the life out of poor Simon. I think he was beginning to see that she was unstable, but he thought Hilary should also have understood that and made allowances. But it was Gillian's own nature which was her undoing. She wanted to be better than she ever could be, and when she found out that it was beyond her, she could not take it. She hadn't got the gift to lift her above the ordinary, you see. Photography is difficult. You need to be a certain type of genius for that.'

'So she took some pills,' said Dorna.

'I'm sure it was an accident. I think she only took them to frighten people and gain sympathy for herself, but it went tragically wrong. Simon has lived with it for years, but the first bit of real interest he has shown in another girl was when he looked at your photograph. I could see it immediately on his face, and in his eyes as he handed it back to me. In fact, he asked if he could keep it, and I said he could. It was like giving him something very precious. I had high hopes of that, Dorna. Was I wrong?'

Dorna bit her lip, forcing back the tears.

'I expect so,' she said, huskily. 'I don't think anything will come of it, Liz. By the way, do you know a girl called Sylvia Parrish?'

Liz frowned and shook her head.

'Can't say I do. Who is she?'

'A friend of Simon's.'

'Ah well, it looks like I don't know everything about him after all, doesn't it? By the way, Hilary says you haven't been to see her yet. She has been trying to reach you by telephone, as I have. Where have you been?'

'Hiding from my cousin's young friends,' said Dorna, ruefully. 'I couldn't get any work done otherwise.'

'Well, don't forget to go and see her when you can spare the time.'

'I can spare the time,' Dorna agreed.

She thought about the telephone calls as she walked home from the nearest Underground station. In her briefcase she carried two more projects from Liz Paige, both of which would be easier to fulfil than that of Hilary Grant.

Had Simon been calling her, by any chance? Had she missed hearing his voice?

She sighed and let herself into the flat. At least she still had work to do.

CHAPTER FIFTEEN

The flow of visitors to the flat began to ease off, and Dorna also had to cope with another visit from Mark who had been forced to leave his temporary accommodation and was finding difficulty in obtaining something else suitable.

'It would be so simple if we got married as we had planned, Dorna,' he insisted. 'You must realize I am serious about this now. I have to be in London for a few months, then I may be going to Canada. You could come with me on a delayed honeymoon.'

'I'm sorry, Mark,' she said, almost desperately, 'I *told* you, I love someone else.'

'Who doesn't give a hoot for you. Where's your pride?'

She wanted to ask him about his pride which had always been so much in evidence, but he was not in a reasonable mood.

Then Dorna began to grow angry. She had laid aside some intricate work to talk to him, and now she'd had enough.

'Please go, Mark,' she said, quietly, 'and don't come back. I don't wish to see you again.'

'You really mean it,' he said, after looking at her closely.

'I don't love you, Mark, not any more. It really is finished.'

Scowling he turned and made for the door. 'I hope you won't be sorry one day, Dorna.'

'I hope so, too.'

Yet when the door had closed finally behind Mark, she found that her hands were trembling too much for work, and she sat for a while massaging her fingers. The bell rang again, and Dorna decided to ignore it. If Mark had come back, she certainly did not want another argument.

It rang imperiously, and insistently for a third time, and with a sigh she went to the door.

'I knew you were in,' said Simon Elliott. 'I saw you showing your boyfriend out of the door. Why didn't you tell me about him, Dorna? It would have saved a lot of time and heartache. I would have known not to get involved. Now ... now I couldn't leave again without seeing you.'

'Simon!'

She could hardly speak his name, but stood aside weakly as he walked into the room, then she leaned against the door.

'Nice,' he said, appreciatively. 'Smells of lemons. Better than last time I came. It was full of teenagers then.'

She followed him into the sittingroom and flopped into a chair. Her legs were trembling so much that she did not want him to see.

'My cousin Alison and her friends were here. She has been sent home to her mother, my Aunt Claire,' Dorna told him. 'I couldn't work with Alison in the room.'

'Ah yes ... work,' he repeated. 'I suppose your friend who left a few minutes ago doesn't mind leaving you to get on with your work.'

'He *was* my friend,' Dorna admitted. 'We were engaged to be married, but it's all over now. It was all over before I went to Egypt.'

She asked Simon to sit down, but he continued to stand, then to wander around picking up objects and putting them down. She felt so nervous that she hardly knew what to say. Why had he come? Why did he want to see her?

'What went wrong, Dorna? Didn't he want a career girl? Was it too much for him after all?'

'He certainly didn't want me,' she admitted. 'He wanted the daughter of an industrialist who was going to employ him ... or he thought he wanted her. Something went wrong. I suspect it was not quite as he had hoped, so he came back to me, but...'

'But?' he prompted, after he had turned to

181

look her full in the face.

'I didn't love him,' she whispered. 'I couldn't marry him when I didn't love him.'

'Could you marry me, if you loved me?' he asked, almost harshly. 'Or would you be forever walking out on me and leaving me scrappy notes when it suited you?'

'And what about you!' she flashed. 'What about your private affairs? I was soon put to one side when that Mrs Parrish came on the telephone.'

'Get your coat on,' he commanded.

She was taken aback. 'I'm sorry, but I don't see...'

'I said to put your coat on,' he repeated. 'I'm going to take you to meet the Parrishes—Sylvia, Peter, five-year old Norma and the youngest child, Simon, who is my godson. The poor little scrap was taken to hospital with a suspected spinal injury after a fall. Sylvia was my secretary for years, and Peter is one of our technicians. Last time I saw her in Cairo, she was hurrying away to telephone home. She did that every night and she often felt uneasy about Simon. But Peter kept telling her not to worry. They were all okay, so she stayed on to finish the work she had to do.

'Then she got a different kind of message. She's psychic, that girl, though it wasn't hard to guess the boy would get into mischief of some kind. He's a menace and Peter ought to give him a good hiding more often. At any rate

Simon fell against their rather old-fashioned fireplace in the drawing room, and injured his back. He's okay now, though. He'll live.'

'Oh, I'm so glad,' cried Dorna. 'I thought...'

'Yes, I know what you thought. You thought she was my mistress and that I'd got an army of mistresses all lined up. Miss Hilary Grant again. But you might as well know that my past affairs are my own concern and no one else's, Dorna.'

She nodded and avoided his eyes.

'I told you we had to talk, but I wanted to keep any discussion between us for the time when you were in a receptive mood ... a rare occasion, if I may say so. Did Hilary tell you about Gillian?'

He walked towards her, reaching out to take her hands.

'What did she tell you, Dorna?'

'That ... that she had not found Gillian's work satisfactory and had lost her a commission by telling someone ... something of that kind. Gillian was so upset that she took an overdose. Oh Simon, how terrible for you. I didn't think you would want to talk about it.'

'And you thought I was following Hilary about to check up on her?'

'Something of the kind.'

He nodded. 'It took me a long time to get over Gillian. I blamed myself more than Hilary. I should have seen her career meant everything to her, and tried to help her every way I could.'

'But it wasn't your fault surely,' she whispered. 'I mean, she had you to think about and to love her. That should have been enough for any girl.'

'Would it have been enough for you, Dorna? Hilary advised me to come and see you and not be put off by anything until we talked it out. I went to see her, you know. You managed to work with her quite well, and you showed me that I shouldn't have blamed her.'

'I don't think any blame should be attached to anyone,' she said, huskily. 'I think you should remember all the good things, the love and the laughter, and forget all the bad. Hilary is older now, and has not always been happy herself. I hope she and I will always be friends, even if we insult one another now and again. She won't ever be a nice old lady.'

He smiled then the hurt was back in his eyes as he looked at her.

'I've seen you twice now with the other chap, and I've telephoned without success, and when I called I was entertained by some ear-blasting pop music without sight of you in your own home. But here I am, back again. I would come every day if I thought you loved me as much as I love you. Because if you do, then nothing else matters, nothing at all. I loved you the first time I set eyes on you and that was only a photograph. That is why I followed you, if you must know. I had to be sure you were okay. I couldn't help myself. And later, after I had followed you through the streets of Cairo and spoke to you for the first time, I knew I had not been wrong. I knew that never again would I love anyone as I love you. I might have to settle for a bit of you, after you've laid aside your paintbrushes, but I'd rather have that than nothing.'

Dorna's tears had begun to flow and she mopped them away, quickly.

'What a fool I am,' she said, thickly. 'I never did cry at weddings, but now that I'm so happy I can't believe it's really happening, the tears are dripping all over the place. Oh Simon darling, I do love you, I do. I love you more than my paintbrushes or anything else. I'll always put you first. I promise. My career will *never* mean more to me than you do.'

She was in his arms, and he was kissing her so that her heart hammered, then steadied, and her body seemed to surge with love and passion for him. She had never thought of herself as a passionate woman, but now she knew she was capable of great depth of feeling, but only for Simon.

'We'll be married at once,' he said, playing with a soft silky curl. 'I don't want to wait for you a minute longer than I need. Will you want a quiet wedding, darling, or will it have to be a grand affair? I'll settle for either so long as the bride is my Dorna.'

'A quiet wedding, I think,' she said, happily,

'though my mother and stepfather will want to come. Also Aunt Claire, Uncle Frank and ... Oh Lord ... Alison! Liz Paige, of course. What about you? I don't even know your relatives, Simon.'

'Liz Paige, certainly, and my parents who live in Norfolk. They are going to love you. Oh, and an invitation we have to deliver in person.'

'To whom?'

'Hilary Grant, of course. I suspect a soft centre there, and she might even cry at our wedding. That would be something to see.'

Simon had leaned his chin on her hair, and now he tilted her face to kiss her again. Dorna was transported with joy. She had never known that love could be so wonderful, if the right man came along.

'Let's go out to dinner and celebrate,' Simon said against her hair. 'Let's go somewhere which reminds us of Egypt.'

'I don't need anything else to remind me of Egypt,' said Dorna, happy and contented as a kitten. 'After all, I have you.'

Library at Home Service
Community Services
Hounslow Library, CentreSpace
24 Treaty Centre, High Street
Hounslow TW3 1ES

WORKING IN PARTNERSHIP WITH

0	1	2	3	4	5	6	7	8	9
3080			993	624	885	846	387	808	
6 70	801	7862	653			876	507	638	
	611		303	864		666	127		
	901	9772			3325		3087		
			1663		9525	706			
7670						806	9507	586	
					845				
								1928	

P10-L2061